# WHEN SHE COMES KNOCKING

DAN MCDOWELL

Black Rose Writing | Texas

First printing



ISBN: 978-1-68513-226-2
PUBLISHED BY BLACK ROSE WRITING
www.blackrosewriting.com

Printed in the United States of America
Suggested Retail Price (SRP) $19.95

Editor: Mark Levesque
Cover Art/Author Photo: Tiffiny McDowell

*When She Comes Knocking* is printed in EB Garamond

For everyone, but not just anyone.

# WHEN SHE COMES KNOCKING

*"Any fool can make things more complex. It takes a touch of genius to move in the opposite direction."* – Albert Einstein

*"Good fences make good neighbors."* – Robert Frost

*"Love your neighbor as yourself."* – Leviticus 19:18

# MERGERS AND ACQUISITIONS

An e-mail notification popped up on my laptop.

*Hello,*

*Welcome to Olkov Enterprises. We want your transition into the organization to be seamless. Your current personnel files and records with J&P will be merged. We're pleased to announce we are honoring your tenure. You've been selected based on a preset rationale and record of salesmanship that supersedes that of your peers. Please keep this matter confidential until the divestiture is complete.*

*Congratulations, and welcome to the Olkov family!*

*Sincerely yours,*

*Mori Olkov, CEO*

It hadn't even been a minute before Bob Dowdy from accounting knocked on my door in a syncopated rhythm.

"Hey, Ben, you got a minute?" he asked, raising his thick eyebrows up and down a couple of times.

I minimized my e-mail window but didn't look up.

"Ben..."

Reaching into my desk drawer, I pretended to busy myself as I pulled out a stapler and mumbled. "Barge right in... why don't you?"

"Huh?"

I let him sweat.

"This isn't funny," he said, coming around my desk and grabbing one of my red sticky notes.

I sighed, closing the lid to my laptop.

He went back to the opposite side of my desk, grabbing a pen and writing something on it.

"Alright," I said. "What's so urgent that can't wait?"

He slid the sticky note across to me.

*OLKOV ? ? ?*

I shrugged and shook my head.

"I guess you haven't heard, then?" he asked, standing up and closing the door.

"Heard what?"

His voice dropped to a whisper. "Middletown's being divested."

"Divested?" I said, gulping for dramatic effect.

"Yep. The Russians own us now."

"So, what happens?"

"4.3% of us keep a job. The rest walk out of here with a pink slip and a box."

"Wow... I thought we were doing alright."

"Yeah, I'm just waiting for my e-mail," he said, checking his smartphone. "Damn spam blocker's probably got it in quarantine. I'll be alright. Yep... Old Bob-o's a people person. Unlike some of us... You're a good guy, Ben. I'm sure you'll find your way."

Bob propped his feet on my desk.

"Don't," I said, opening my laptop and logging back in.

"Well?" he asked.

"How'd you find out about this?"

"I was messing around in the breakroom and heard two of the execs chatting."

"Well, tell me about these Olkov guys?"

"Look 'em up," he said. "See what you can find."

I clicked around on my laptop and keyed it in. Scrolling through several websites, I found little.

"It all looks generic, ambiguous, and fake, Bob."

"Whatever, man, thought you'd want to know," he said, walking out of the room. "Good luck."

I checked my watch. Shift end was just ahead, and I was ready to call it a day.

At J&P we sold pills, the kind that addicted people. The ones that made them come back until the medicine owned them or they died. These were honest to God tragedies, but at some point, it's just business, working on commission. Figures on a spreadsheet, nothing more, nothing less. You dehumanized them, so they weren't husbands, brothers, daughters, or wives. They were clients — sources of income for people like you and me.

I'll admit, I have issues, and they kind of wind me up inside. That's where my crazy becomes yours, a hint of deception often the glue bonding us together.

My theory? Life gets windy, and when we're blown restless through the sky, our feet end up on the ground or in it, but that choice is ours to make. The path to which I'm headed. The path to which we're all headed. Lots of smart people think they know about the things that drive people to do and to be — all the nuances that make a person tick. Few understand what makes us break.

# GREENER PASTURES

I laid a couple of Chinese takeout containers on the kitchen table and sat down across from Hannah. Despite the diffused lighting and soft jazz, I didn't get the mood right. It was hot, and the dining area ceiling fan squeaked. And I don't mean a cute little chirp, but such a shrill noise, you preferred to sweat at meal times. I'd put off repairing it too long. There was a part of me aware enough to know if I tried, it would quickly end up collapsed and dismembered on the floor.

We split date nights between therapy and catch-ups every other Tuesday. Our son, Davey, was six, and my father-in-law, Hal, had taken him for the night. Hannah and I needed time to calibrate. You know, to avoid common couple conundrums.

Hannah studied me for a moment and sighed. "Chow Fung's again?"

I nodded.

"That's the third time this week."

"Second. Monday didn't count."

"If you want to change your fortune, try a magic 8-Ball," she said, crushing a fortune cookie in her hand and sliding it across the table.

I wasn't going to let my plan backfire.

"Yeah, an 8-Ball sounds pretty good right now."

"Ben!"

"From all I hear, Garashock makes an 8-Ball look like a half dose of baby aspirin, and I've got a trunk full."

"Ben Decker. Get yourself together."

"I've just been slammed. I'm sorry," I said, searching for a way to improve the plan.

"It's fine. You need to relax."

"How about a little dessert?" I said, pushing the crumbled fortune cookie back toward her. The fortune waited just beneath the crumbs.

She shook her head, her chestnut eyes glaring half an inch below her auburn bangs. "Seriously?"

"Humor me."

"Alright, fine," she said, pulling out the fortune from the crushed-up cookie and looking up at me.

*1737 17^th Street*

"What is this, Ben?"

I pulled a key from my pocket, laying it and my smartphone on the table. There were pictures of a home I'd queued up on a real estate app. It was a beautiful pier and beam craftsman styled place, fully restored.

"Take a look," I said, mustering the best smile I could conjure. "It stood out from the rest."

As she swiped through, zooming in on each image, her eyes told me the historical charm of the place resonated. Its bones were well-aged. The pronounced wood siding showcased an irresistibility that stood out amidst a slew of forgettable brick and stucco lot and blocks across town.

"What do you think?" I asked.

She grinned. "When can we move?" an unfamiliar giddiness in her voice.

"At this price, it's now or never."

"Now, Ben Decker. Let's go now!" she said, laying my smartphone on the table.

I leaned over and kissed her.

"That Lo-Mein breath..." she said.

"Well, at least we match."

"Can we afford it?"

"Can we afford not to?"

We locked eyes, I took her by the hand, and we ran to the front door.

# FRESH START

Our nighttime cruise in the Mercedes became an adventure.

Middletown, our micropolitan behemoth of a town, was twenty-eight miles, east to west, and had 49,827 residents within the city limits proper. We had a bit of everything. Although the exaggerated sprawl left us isolated from the rest of Texas, we were surprisingly corporate — to the point of having multiple big box stores, billboards for hire, and our own local television and radio stations.

Hannah and I bantered back and forth with the top down. Foreigner told us what love was. And our future came into frame.

"1737," I said, pulling into the driveway.

The house was staged and ready for our arrival.

"Well, no one can say this place isn't lit well," Hannah said. "It's pretty at night."

"Yeah. It sure is," I said.

We stepped out of the car and walked up toward the house.

She took me by the hand. "That wraparound porch, Ben! I can see the rocking chairs now. Coffee... watching the world go by... late night chats... Davey in the yard playing."

I smiled. "That sounds great."

I pulled out the key, unlocking the red front door, it's bronzed knocker just below the peephole.

Cueing up my best real estate agent voice, I gave the pitch like the guy did for me the previous day with an added Yankee accent to match his. "Original wood floors, every light equipped with dimmer switches, not to mention ceiling fans to combat the lingering summer heat, a classic homeowner's dream breathing modern air, all the while maintaining antiquated charm..."

Hannah looked at me for a second, pulling me toward her. "You're kind of cute when you try. I like your antiquated charm!"

We hadn't flirted like that in months. I missed it. Walking through each of the rooms, our feet echoed as the floors creaked and buckled beneath.

"It's a lot more sweeping than vacuuming," I said. "You good with that?"

"Yeah, but they're beautiful, and you can help, can't you? The scuff marks show the age... and the history. I like it."

"Character marks," I replied. "And the high ceilings? What do you think?"

"They're great. And no popcorn to scrape off them either."

"Thank God. I didn't think we'd ever get that vacuumed up, but your effort was... admirable."

We moved into the front bedroom. The textured walls gave it a modern look. I clunked my fist against one a few times. "Pretty solid. Davey's room?"

"Yeah, I think so," she said, resting her hands in the back of her blue jean pockets as she studied the windows looking onto the front porch. "I'm glad you found it."

"Me, too."

She struggled to close the creaking door to the bedroom.

I looked toward the large row of bay windows in the dining area and then back at Hannah. "Inspector says it's not quite level, but that's alright." I rocked the bedroom door back and forth. "Heavy. They don't make them like they used to," I said, kissing Hannah on the cheek. She loved affection in random moments.

My phone rang. "I've got to take this. Feel free to explore."

"I'm glad to have your permission," she snarked.

"Classic Ben Decker fail," I muttered, stepping into the other room.

Hannah shook her head. Her beauty wasn't just a matter of physical features, but that she was real, raw, and emotional; jagged around the edges, and always managing a sweet, frothy foam of hospitality with the people that mattered most. I loved that about her. That contrast was God's gift to both of us because she could rip me a new one when necessary but offered a delicate touch in all the right moments, too. I needed both.

The call was forgettable, a bunch of rambling about closing a deal with a new pill mill on the west side. I hung up the phone and found my way toward the back of the house and into its master bedroom. It had a nice claw-footed bathtub, his and her sinks, a walk-in shower, and three sets of lights showcasing the developer's ambitious efforts to update it.

Hannah stood there quietly; her eyes fixed on the mirror. She wasn't admiring herself, but in a transcendental space I couldn't articulate. The look was foreign, especially that night.

"Beautiful mother. Stunning wife," I said, my voice getting throaty. "And just back there, you and me..." I clicked my tongue and nodded my head toward the bedroom. "We'll get that floor double reinforced, and make some memories, too, won't we?"

There was no reaction. Hannah's face remained blank, and I couldn't reach her. Reaching people, that's kind of my thing — you have to. Otherwise, you never really connect.

I didn't shun the silence. We were reeling in our own ways for different reasons.

"Are you okay, honey?" I asked.

She looked over at me. "Yeah," she said, punching me in the arm playfully. "You bet we will."

"We'll what?"

"Get the floor reinforced."

"Oh, right, right!"

I held her long and hard. It was the kind of hug that spoke volumes, reassuring that we'd love each other well, like the best friends we were meant to be. Something inside told me to shut up and be present. It was intimate, and somewhere in that moment, I knew we'd arrived home.

We trotted into the main living area, peeking out the west windows. As for 1739, the house next door, it was dark enough not to pay attention to its condition, but its challenges would soon be impossible to ignore. There was a light shining through one of the windows. The curtains were drawn, but only slightly, and they were a little off-center. A silhouetted shadow stood just behind; the motions resemblant to a person scrubbing plates.

"Check it out," I said, pointing toward the window.

"What is it?"

"I saw someone. It seemed like they were watching."

"Okay? Maybe because they live there?" she said, rolling her eyes. She turned around and went in the other room.

I focused on the window for a second before the curtains closed abruptly and the lights went out.

Walking back through the house, we gave each of the rooms another glance, painting pictures in our minds about how we might decorate, what furniture would go where, and so on.

"Alright," I said, peeking out into the moonlit backyard. "This looks nice, too. The covered patio."

"I love it," she said, leaning in to kiss me.

We moved toward the front of the house and peered out the front window. An old wood-paneled station wagon zoomed by unexpectedly. Its obnoxious backfire echoed down the block.

# CORPORATE MAN

Olkov kept one floor of J&P's office tower downtown and it was inevitably the one in the worst shape. They promised to improve things in due time but considering the company's humble roots and dated practices still lingering across mainframes, systems, and personnel, it would be an uphill battle. Commissions were down. Notoriety was up.

In slower moments, it was challenging not to contemplate the toxicity lingering in the campus's air and if it had a lasting effect on my health and well-being. Sometimes I thought it might.

Then came the aesthetic changes. On our floor, they took down the entry sign with the gold-plated J&P branding, replacing it with a silver-toned Olkov logo. Unfortunately, the rent-a-cop sitting under the sign for J&P somehow kept a job as a third-party contractor and between us, I hated that guy. He was annoying, just some thug with a criminal record that couldn't hack it as a real cop. This joker came in to tell us when we breached company policies every chance he had. I could have fallen in line if he did, but a little online snooping and I knew *his* secret. That bag of doobies in the back seat of his Daihatsu left him locked up for a year in the late 80s, and though it was expunged, it was there for prying eyes like mine that paid the $4.99 Neighborbuddy subscription fee to find out.

Don't get the rose-colored glasses out just yet. Our office was still corporate, unwelcoming, and fluorescent as ever, as unnatural a place as you could imagine.

Walls and walls of ugly gray fabric-covered cubicles.

Misaligned Formica tabletops screwed together by our stoner for a groundskeeper.

Ficus trees jammed in every corner.

And that damn water machine. It was always broken or empty.

Life could only come full circle with an unnecessary helping of Bob Dowdy, who was also saved from the layoffs. When he got the e-mail his job was saved, the entire floor halted operations for a moment because of his obnoxious scream. I wasn't about to check on him, though. People say a little of something goes a long way, and as far as Bob and I were concerned, walking the same hallway was more than enough. Apparently, he cooked the books well. He was just a walking, talking HR violation. I didn't want to be guilty by association. People get fired for that.

The good news, limited personnel didn't stop J&P's top selling medication, Garashock, from coming over to Olkov. Things started well, but eventually, Olkov's inexperience in supply chain economics and FDA workflows left scarce quantities of what we deemed "the other little blue pill." The addicts were raging. No matter the press received, good, bad, or ugly, it was all free. And that perhaps was the genius of Olkov.

There was a minor problem. Garashock had to be modified because of proprietary ingredients. We rebranded it as Garashock 500, an inferior pill that cost half the price but flew lower on the FDA radar as a non-opioid. In small doses, it worked miracles on injured backs, swollen necks, and aging hips, but at higher doses, there was no denying its potency and highly addictive nature.

It was the perfect combination of holistic, medicinal, and herbal cocktails packed into pills. The cure to the world's worst ailments, and a cash grab for companies like mine who'd shirked FDA standards for years because of loopholes in the system that allowed them to hand medicine out in large experimental trials. Thanks to those loopholes, the black market grew.

Our lead scientists and board regularly argued that Garashock's traceability on toxicology reports was both a pro and a con. It was marketable to the addicts, but concurrently an unspoken threat. It cured some, while others died on the superhighway to pleasure. I suppose that's the trouble with any great drug in the wrong hands. When people died, the toxicology testing was a struggle during trials. The screenings always turned up negative for any sort of damning active ingredients. Despite being a common denominator in wrongful death suits, there was simply no way to trace it. They talked and talked about ways to amend it, but greed trumped care, and ultimately, nothing was added.

I unscrewed my aspirin, emptying its contents on my desk and pulling out a pill pack of the Garashock 500s. Dropping each of the little blue pills into the bottle, I left one out, picking it up.

I studied it for a second. You'd have to be brain-dead to take a Garashock 500, especially if you knew what was in it. I guess that's where I was.

The losses itemized on my paystub were enough to lead any man to chase his sorrows away.

"And he takes the blue pill," I said, popping the medicine in my mouth.

I will admit, the power of suggestion can expedite the effect of anything, but within a matter of ninety seconds, numbers danced in circles on my screen and my office went into a tailspin. I kept blinking my eyes and shaking my head left to right, hoping to jar myself loose from the self-induced haze. It was the first time I caved. I watched the second hand on the gold-plated Seth Thomas mounted above my door. It started floating, then it came out six inches toward me. Time moved faster, then slower, then faster, and I mellowed out.

My eyes drifted to the TV in the corner of the office. Truth is, I am some kind of movie buff, a cinephile. I keep one on every chance I get. Life gets dull. Work ten years someplace, anyplace... and the meetings, the people, the everything, they all start to look and sound the same. You don't hate them. You don't love them. You just know them.

I played it smart. To sweeten my deal with Olkov, I begged for that TV, and they actually gave me one. That might be a fib of sorts. I negotiated. They provided it to me on the condition I donated 3,472 DVDs and Blu-rays from my personal collection to Olkov for employee use. We had a little closet. Bob Dowdy kept writing "Ben-Buster" on a sheet of paper and taping it on the door, but the cleaning people kept taking it down. The blue and yellow markers added a nice touch.

Hannah was thrilled to free up the cabinet space at home. It would take me some time, though. I wasn't ready to ditch them for streaming or imagine Bob taking one home and scratching it up before he returned it. There was just something about the physical copy. Movies go into a black hole, and then once they're impossible to find, some goof finds a way to bootleg it and sell it to you for exorbitant amounts on eBay. Trust me. My only regret was *Tron*, which cost $79 at a time when it was pulled from the shelves. And here we are now, and you can get it for less than a Route 44 at the Gas 'n Sip.

*Scarface* played in the background that day. Somewhere in the back of my mind, Tony Montana was cursing me because I was high on my own supply. I savored the rush.

*Maybe Tony was my role model.*

*Maybe I was Tony.*

I thought I could enjoy the ride all the way to shift end because I'd had no disruptions the entire day.

Coming down from my ecstasy, there was a tap on the door, my paranoia hitting worse than six cups of coffee in an hour. This side-effect of Garashock 500 was stimulating, troublesome, and well-documented, but our experts had found no way to resolve it, instead opting for the added black label warning on the package. Hyper focus had its benefits, but the paranoia, man, did it wear me out. I raked the loose aspirin into my desk drawer in a rush, closing down an unfinished round of solitaire and dropping the pill bottle with the 500s in my work bag. Looking productive as ever, I clicked around a spreadsheet, pivoting sales figures.

Click.

Clack.

Click.

Print.

Mori Olkov was at the door. I waved him in.

"Come in, sir. Good to see you."

He smiled. "Catch you at a bad time, Ben?"

My reaction was nothing but plastic — cheap imitation plastic. "Oh, no, no. Not at all, sir."

I sharpened a pencil on my desk and pulled a sales report from the printer.

Mori sat down, still grinning, his teeth a perfect candidate for a small-market dental commercial — anything bigger than that, maybe not.

"You got a minute?" he asked.

The chit-chat and repetition annoyed me. I was ready for him to tell me what he was there for. His presence was more an intrusion than anything, but he was the CEO. He could pop in because he paid me to listen, to have a minute for him, to do whatever he needed me to.

His accent was smooth with occasional English language failures. That made him more endearing. He was tall and handsome, thick hair graying at the temples, blue eyes complimentary of his Russian roots. That day, he wore a blue-checkered business suit that was the perfect match to his sturdy frame. Don't worry. I'd never tell you that the blazer came from Brooks Brothers, or that it complemented a tie from Pronto Uomo, or that his belt color was a mauve number from Ralph Lauren when it should have been a burnt orange from the US Polo Association. I'm not that degree of sophisticated. Nor do I think boring you with such detail is worth the time (This in mind, the commentary should suffice.). It makes you sound slightly less crazy. That's half the battle. You make yourself sound a little less crazy than the rest to sell your point.

I nodded at Mori, dropping my horn-rimmed glasses on the desk, my mind plummeting from the Garashock as it raced through me. It all happened within ten minutes. I understood why we had so many repeat clients. The effect of the pill was satisfying, a dopamine hit like no other.

I'd only had a few meetings with Mori, all positive and to my benefit. Problem was, they were directionless. If he was kingpin of the Olkov empire, he was by far the most pleasant sort of man I could envision in such a role. We'd converse for hours. Forget the tropes on TV. This guy was a real boss, demanding respect without flexing a physical muscle. But there was work to be done, and if I didn't keep him on target, I'd often have to steer him back on course.

"To what do I owe the pleasure, sir?"

"Ben, I live by simple motto," he said, with a thick accent. "Shoot straight. Make money. Do these well, you succeed."

"That's great, Mori. Straight and to the point! Just my kind of thing."

"And yours?" he asked.

"Its... uh... it's to make Olkov Enterprises look good."

"Fair enough."

I'd ad-libbed and we both knew it. Still, somewhere within, it annoyed me that four words could be the thesis statement of a CEO. I envied him, because no matter how hard I tried, my own was at least four-hundred forty-four, and any efforts to shorten it would just make it longer.

I ran my finger down the report, waiting for him to declare a more intentional purpose for his arrival. He kept the pleasantries going, probably to butter me up for some other request.

"It's great to be working with you. We're happy to join... to help the hurting, to heal them. So many things good we do to change the world, yeah? Hmm-hmm," he said, a habitual laugh to follow.

The laugh was one that reassured me. I knew somewhere behind his pleasant façade, it was also textbook Mori. The Mori Olkov stamp of approval told a guy he was in the "in" crowd. I would do whatever it took to stay in good graces. That was the path to success. I struggled to find words as I nodded, slipping away as unspeakable psychosis overwhelmed me again from the 500 pill.

The room's walls caved in. Mori's face became more striking before it bent in contorted circles, the fluorescent lights growing vibrant, my skin crawling. I had no prior experience with the effects of either iteration of Garashock, only the secondhand recounting from clients. Continuing to revel in the moment, I was as much bewildered as I was intrigued.

"Yes. It's a great opportunity to partner. The market's hot. Once we get things moving again, I see a profitable season," I said, mustering words quicker than my state of mind should have allowed.

Mori pulled a Cuban cigar from his jacket pocket, handing me another. He lit his first.

"Mori, we can't..."

"Can't what?" he said, taking a drag and puffing it in the air, toward one of our non-working smoke detectors. The cheap bastards at J&P never paid to repair it, and I hadn't told Olkov either. Worked out, I guess.

"That rent-a-cop downstairs will have us for lunch."

"You think I care? Who's paying bills around here? Me or him?" he said, puffing it again. "I've got many ideas to grow company, Ben. Bigger and better! I want you to help," he said, his voice having an underwater sort of quality. "Olkov will be good to you if you're good to us."

"Thanks, Mori. I'll save this for a celebratory moment," I said, putting the cigar in my desk drawer.

"Oh, Ben, loosen up, my friend. This *is* celebratory moment!"

I nodded, slower than usual, but he didn't know me well enough to differentiate. Sweat rolled down the back of my neck as I struggled to swallow and grabbed at the sides of my chair.

Mori studied me, his eyes widening. "You okay, buddy? What's going on?"

I sipped my water bottle and sighed, praying for relief. It wasn't happening.

"Mori, I'm sorry. I think I... I need to excuse myself for a break. I'll swing by your office in a few minutes, and we can chat some more."

"Just make sure to wash your hands with soap... and water, huh? Hmm-hmm," he said.

I struggled to walk a straight line as I stood and approached the door, my knees nearly buckling to the floor.

Mori reached out, patting me on the shoulder. "Are you okay there, Ben? Can I get you some help? You need an ambulance... or AA?"

I don't think he meant to be cold. He was making light to ease my anxieties, but it did me no good. The pill did everything for me and then some.

"I'm fine, just feeling... faint. A splash of water ought to fix me up," I said, mumbling as the room continued to spin. I grabbed the handle and let myself out.

"Alright," he said, adjusting his suspenders at the belt line. "I'll be in my office. Time to lay off happy sauce at lunch hour, huh? Hmm-hmm."

I found my way into a men's room stall, losing my composure again — some uncommon anxiety eating away at me, the sick cancer it was. The dark nature of the pill took hold as I studied the stall door and my world melted away. Its gray metal oozed to the floor.

I saw Dad. He was in the backyard, threading the weed eater, explaining how to use it as he crushed another beer can and pitched it over the neighbor's fence. Taking me along the fence line, he pull-started it, triggering it a few times, hacking blades of grass that overstayed their welcome.

"Go for it, bud," he said, opening and swilling another beer.

I took it from him and pulled the trigger. Something startled me and the line dug into the dirt.

"Aren't you worth anything, kid? Damn!" he said, slapping me across the face.

A flush in the neighboring stall brought me back.

"Ben, you okay in there?" Mori called from outside the door. "I'm not going to wait. I want to make sure you're not dead."

"Yes, sir," I said, taking a deep breath. "All good."

And though part of me was lying, the other meant it, because in that moment, peace met pleasure. Ben Decker, Sales Rep, was inches away from Ben Decker, VP of Sales — triple the money, quadruple the opportunity.

Mori could have chosen plenty of others that worked in the office, but he picked *this* loser. After washing my hands, I studied my reflection. I pointed at the mirror, mimicking Mori's accent. "Shoot straight. Make money. Shoot straight. Make money."

Another stall door popped open. I'd misjudged thinking I was alone. It was Bob Dowdy. He laughed, clicking his tongue twice, and patted me on the back with his unwashed hands as he went out the door.

"Keep it up, Decker."

*Still a loser, Ben.*

# READY OR NOT, HERE WE COME

The screen door squeaked. A brawny, ponytailed woman emerged from behind, pulling it open. She kept the bolt bar engaged, leaving a four-inch gap for us to speak.

"Yeah, I'm sorry," she said. "I... I don't do solicitors. Do I know you?"

Hannah grinned. "Hi! Don't worry! We're not solicitors. We're your new neighbors. I'm Hannah. This is Ben, and our son, Davey."

"Give me a minute," she said, slamming the door shut.

I shook my head. This was going exactly like I had envisioned. Exactly.

"I think we should have waited, 'til move in day at least," I mumbled.

"What's life without neighbors?" Hannah asked.

"Better," I said.

"Don't be a bump on a log."

"Fine."

I looked over at the driveway and smirked, nodding my head toward the wood-paneled station wagon. "Buick Roadmaster. I haven't seen one of those since I was a kid."

"I guess those car magazine subscriptions finally paid off, then?" Hannah asked.

"You know I have a thing for hardbodies," I said, nudging her with my elbow.

She punched me in the arm.

1739 17th Street had an accumulating list of grievances. Yet somehow, the situation felt poetic, a lost parable. A tale of matching houses built with the same materials, standing side by side for a century, the first, immaculate and preserved, the second having worn out its welcome years earlier.

The home was terribly unlevel, a true environmental risk. Its exterior paint was outdated and sunbaked, lacking cohesive styling as it peeled away from the wood, screaming for a fresh coat. The lone consistency in the place's exterior was the green foliage emerging from the east side, courtesy of unkempt vines creeping up toward the attic vents. Just adjacent, squirrels and birds entered and exited the greenery through a row of burrowed notches and holes that overtook portions of dilapidated wood. As for the yard, it was abysmal, packed with long-forgotten furniture, garbage, and eclectic mementos hinting at the place's past. Though Hannah and I were purchasing the corner lot, only fifty-five steps would separate our homes, and she was right. We owed it to ourselves to meet the resident. It was opinions on the timing and initiation of the encounter where we differed. There was no denying it would take time to close the disparities between the properties.

"Wow! Did you see that?" Davey yelled, kicking up a clod of dirt as a deflated soccer ball soared through the air. A pack of roaches scattered from a hollow point in the base of the front yard's dying pecan tree as the ball collided and the critters rushed under the house. The grassless yard had no character, only remnants of lingering death. True, the drought had been unkind through the summer, but I found it curious how the irrigation system at the place right next door could keep the St. Augustine blades so immaculate. Maybe it was love and care. Or, perhaps, a disregard for community watering restrictions. Either way, I was thankful. It was the little things that created tangible value and would make us more at home. Who was I to get bent out of shape if the developer over-watered to keep it nice before the sale?

"Davey, stop that!" I said as our son swung from the tree's lowest branch. It snapped. "Dad gum it, son!"

There was a commotion at the door again.

"Just a minute," the woman's frazzled voice called from the other side. "I've got to finish up."

I nodded. As we waited, I checked my phone and sighed, looking over both shoulders. I noticed Hannah studying the disheveled front porch, its broken rocking chairs, cracked windows, and a paint bucket full of smashed Marlboros. Meanwhile, Davey weaseled his way back up the tree on another limb, clinging for dear life — the limb, not Davey.

"What's the matter?" she asked.

I sighed, tucking my phone away. "Nothing. Just a contract I'm trying to firm up. The client keeps e-mailing... You know, we must have caught this lady at a bad time. Why don't we come back later?"

"Why are you so... squirmy?" she asked. "You're usually pretty good at meeting new people."

"It's etiquette, Hannah. You always let the neighbor make the first..."

"Move!" the woman called out gruffly to a yapping mutt, pulling the door open partially. "Yeah. I heard the place finally sold... Well, good for you. Great for you."

"Yes!" Hannah said, grinning.

A small Shih Tzu came around the corner, nipping at the back of her leg and barking at us. "Get back, Gonzo!" she yelled in a gruff voice that rattled the windows.

"I love puppies," Davey said.

"You do? The friggin' thing just did a no-no on my hardwood floor," she said, studying each of us closer, a sort of squint in her eyes. She unhinged the bolt and pulled the door open, shooing the mutt to the side with her bare foot. "Come in," she said, pushing the door closed before Davey could catch up. Her faded white t-shirt and gray shorts did nothing to accentuate her figure. "Don't want to let all the cool air out," she continued. Her eyes widened at Hannah as if she were lecturing.

"Come on, Davey," I called out, a harshness in my voice.

He darted up the steps and grabbed onto Hannah's arm. As we followed her through the door into the living room, the woman pointed to a brown leather couch.

"Make yourself at home," she said, hastily walking toward the kitchen. There was a sort of hiccup in her gait. The aged floor buckled beneath as she moved toward the house's rear. Picking up the dog, the woman sighed loudly.

"Why's this place so messy?" Davey asked, much louder than I would have preferred.

I grabbed his arm pulling him closer. "Shut up and be respectful. If you don't have anything good to say..."

"Don't say it at all," he said, finishing my sentence.

"Good. Thank you, son."

The woman made a glass of water for herself in the sink.

"Momma can't keep a place nice if she tries. Can she?" she said, talking to the dog like a small child. She carried the dog into the back bedroom, saying something unintelligible to the mutt.

"There's plenty of work around here for 'momma' to do," I said, grumbling under my breath.

Hannah glared. "Ben, if you don't have anything good to say..."

Davey jumped from the couch, heading toward the room the woman had gone into. Hannah took me by the hand as I struggled to stay calm. I was out of my element from the moment I stepped inside.

"Get over here and sit down!" I demanded.

Davey teetered across the room, bouncing onto the sofa as a large puff of dust particles filled the air and choked us up.

"Stop that," Hannah said, coughing and clearing her throat.

"Why's it so dusty?" he asked. "Does she need a maid?"

I grabbed his arm again. "Not another word!" I said, my teeth clenched.

A television in the dining room blared a *Jerry Springer* rerun, the censor beeping and blurring more than was intelligible. A TV dinner sat on the table next to a crossword puzzle. I was still unsettled; I couldn't get a read.

I struggled with the room's disorder — its lack of styling, further testament to the meandering priorities of a woman long abandoned. A cuckoo clock resting on the fireplace mantel, a hunting rifle gracing the east wall, a Fisherman's Weekly calendar remaining unturned from 2014, and a few Hummels standing, mismatched and kitschy. And in the room's corner sat an unfurled roll-top desk, struggling to hide a large stack of unpaid bills and a stash of Werther's toffee. The home decor didn't match the woman's age. She was younger, forty-seven or forty-eight, but the place looked like it could have belonged to her parents.

Davey reached into the jar on the coffee table, helping himself to a strawberry candy.

"You should ask first," Hannah whispered.

Davey launched the candy into his mouth as fast as she'd spoken, tossing the wrapper on the floor.

"Pick it up," I said harshly.

He darted across the room to the roll-top desk and grabbed a Hummel. "Look, Mom. It's Dopey!"

The door to the back bedroom slammed.

"Put that down!" the woman said as she came back into the room.

"I'm sorry," he said, laying it down. His eyes were glassy as he walked back toward Hannah and me.

I wanted to reiterate to Hannah how much "I told you so," was racing through my head. I kept her hand clasped in mine, and I think somewhere in the friction between our two hands, we knew this visit could have gone better.

"*Antiques Roadshow* says that's worth four grand," the woman said, moving it to a higher shelf next to a cup of pens and composition notebooks. "Been in my family for years. It was my mother's."

I squeezed Hannah's hand, reaffirming our unannounced arrival was a mistake.

The woman turned the television off. "No more advice from Jerry. That's enough. I hear most of them are actors, anyhow."

"Say what?" I asked.

"The ones doing all the biting, scratching, and screaming on the TV," she said, raising her eyebrows.

Muting my reaction was a no-go. Instead, I squinted my eyes and pulled away.

The woman sat down, wiping a bead of sweat from her brow. "I'm Jean. Jean Jackson. Forgive me. I didn't mean to have a tone with your kid. You guys caught me at a bad time. I tell myself every day I'm gonna get rid of the dog, but it hasn't happened yet. Next door, huh?"

"Yeah," Hannah said. "It's beautiful. I love it!"

Jean chortled. "Tch... yeah. Should have seen how bad it was before you got here. The people trashed it. Mother lived there for years before she passed. And she kept it spotless! I miss that."

I looked over at Hannah. With sixteen years together, we didn't always meld, but in a moment like this, the same thought raced through both of our minds. *If only Mother were still here to teach you a thing or two.*

I shook my head. "Some people... Well, it'll be good to know someone that knows the place's history. We promise to take care of it. Don't we, Hannah?"

Hannah smiled. "Of course. Team effort. Go team go!"

I looked at her. I wasn't sure about that last statement, but it had been a while since her spunk had shown. Perhaps I was just out of touch.

Jean locked eyes with me a second longer than natural. "You say that now..."

"Oh?" I asked, studying the woman's face.

Davey took another strawberry candy.

"I'm sorry," Hannah interrupted. "We don't keep a lot of sugar around."

"I lost a tooth," Davey said, pointing to the new one almost grown in.

Jean motioned her hand like all was forgiven. "Yeah, yeah. Did the tooth fairy bring you something nice?"

"A two-dollar bill... I'm a believer!"

She nodded. "I bet you are. I've got a drawer full of those over there. My husband... ex-husband collected them."

"Really? Can I see?"

"Maybe another time, sweetheart," she said, a growing impatience in her voice.

"So, what can you tell us about the neighborhood?" Hannah asked.

"Plenty, I suppose. I've been here my whole life."

"Well, twenty-eight looks good on you," I said.

"You're such a kidder," she said, standing up, raking a few dust bunnies from the coffee table onto the floor and helping herself to a strawberry candy. "I'm tethered here... been my family's for years. Hard times just kept a-comin'. Granddaddy built the house you're moving into, and the rest is... history."

Hannah looked toward me for a moment. "I know old houses always have their stories."

"Sure. Too many to discuss in one sitting, though," Jean said. "A little of this, a little of that. Let's have coffee sometime once you get moved in and we'll chat."

Hannah nodded. "That sounds good."

"Great," I said. "Well, we don't want to interrupt your routine. We better get going. We've got that Meet-the-Teacher night."

Jean grinned at me. The look was uncomfortably long. "I'll bake an apple pie to welcome you."

"That's too sweet," Hannah said, interrupting before I could say anything else. "Ben's favorite."

There's an unspoken code in moments like this where one woman declares to another to stand down. Hannah's glare told Jean all she needed to know.

Down the rear hallway, the dog's barking remained incessant, reminding me why I hate them. They crap. They yap. They do some more. No thanks.

The door popped open and Gonzo dashed to the front, leaping onto Davey.

"He's really sweet, Mommy," Davey said, as the dog licked his face, panting rapidly.

"Yeah, my Gonzo's a sucker for kids. You guys smell good to him," Jean said, looking at the boy.

Davey studied Jean. "Smell good? What do you mean?"

"Yeah. Everybody knows sweaty kids smell like wet dogs."

"Do you like the smell of wet dogs?" he asked.

She chuckled. "Like is a strong word, but I'm used to it," she said, rifling her fingers through our son's sweaty hair. "The best part is Gonzo wouldn't hurt a flea. He might have a few, but he'd never hurt any," she said plucking at him.

We chuckled, her perfect audience on cue.

"Well, we'll catch up with you soon," Hannah said.

I looked at Jean. "We're firming up the closing date, but it'll be here before you know it."

"Great," she said, the tone in her voice growing kinder as she patted Davey on the shoulder. "You're a lucky man, Ben." She smiled at me uncomfortably long. "It'll be good to have some people next door again. I'll just love seeing your perfect little family through my window."

"Well, we've had our hard times, but we're still blessed," I said.

I didn't overthink Jean's statement, but it lingered somewhere in the back of my mind.

Suddenly, Jean wasn't ready for us to leave. We were no longer intruders, but guests.

"You guys from around here?" she asked.

"Yeah. Sort of. We live on the east side," I said, looking back at Hannah and approaching the door.

Hannah glanced toward the empty candy dish. "I'm sorry. I guess we cleaned you out," she said.

Jean chuckled forcefully. "Oh, that's alright. My hips don't need any more of that. That's where it all goes, anyhow."

I smiled.

"What do you mean your hips?" Davey asked.

"I don't know," Jean said, half-joking. "Maybe Mommy can explain calories to you a little better..."

She had a nerve on her, but it seemed consistent and impersonal.

"See you later," I said, corralling my crew to the door.

As Jean moved to let us out, we walked to our black Range Rover parked in the driveway of 1737. A white picket fence divided the homes, but it was only a few feet tall and had its share of broken sections.

Davey waved out the back window as we drove away, his memory of the Hummel incident diffused or erased.

I checked the rear-view mirror as we approached the intersection. Jean stood in front of 1739, her beat-up vehicle covered in tree sap and bird crap. She scratched Gonzo's head, walking back toward the house. I rolled through the stop sign, still contemplating on our visit and her sudden change. A service truck cruised down the block at an excessive speed. It didn't register. Thankfully, Hannah yelled out. I slammed the brakes, that ugly screech surely having left Jean aware of our near mishap. The truck zoomed by, missing us by an angel's fingertip.

"What was that about? Weren't you paying attention?" she asked, taking a deep breath.

"I'm sorry. I guess I was still thinking about the visit," I replied, running my fingers through my hair.

"Well, like most of us, including *you*... I'm sure she's an acquired taste."

"I couldn't get a read on her," I said. "I don't like that."

"You and your 'getting a read.' You act like that's the most important thing a person can do," she said.

I think Hannah was still keyed up from the grief I'd given earlier about going to meet Jean unannounced.

"It is, honey. J&P conditioned and trained me to be a professional observer to make sales. Olkov is reinforcing that with additional techniques. It's all I know to do. That's how we sell. It might seem cold and calculated, but it's real. We're always sending out signals. And whether they're mixed, steady, or blank, there's a lot to understand... layers to dissect. Even this conversation right here. A fly on the wall would pick up on our signals and learn something."

"What do you mean, Daddy?" Davey asked.

I peeked at him in the rear-view and turned the radio down. "I mean that when we talk to and spend time with people, we should be able to understand what makes them tick, how they work, and why. If there's no motivation, then what are they here for? What are we here for?"

I knew that would only lead to another question, but Davey was entitled to those, now more than ever.

"What's motivation?" he asked.

"It's drive," I said. "What gives us purpose. The thing that sparks competition. It helps us to achieve our goals and dreams."

"You're sounding like a motivational speaker," Hannah said, patting me on the shoulder as we continued our cruise back home. The look in her eyes told me my connecting with Davey was all she needed to bury the hatchet.

"I'll start my national tour next week!" I said, smiling.

# INSOMNIA

I couldn't sleep.

Hannah was usually the one burning the midnight oil while I snoozed, but after meeting Jean, our roles reversed, and my sleeping pills were rendered useless. After I struggled through the ending of *Speed 2*, I eased up and turned the program off.

"And that's why I hate sequels," I muttered.

Hannah rolled over and said something unintelligible. She was resting better, and I swore myself up and down I needed to do the same. I had early morning meetings and commitments. We needed to get Davey to school. We were moving.

As I relaxed, the air conditioner to the house turned off, and a jolt coursed through me like an electric shock. The little squiggles resting behind my eyelids were bright and colorful, going from the stark contrast of the TV glow to darkness. I saw Jean's face and a slew of images of our soon to be house, spliced and cut together like a bad home movie as it raced through my imagination.

Her mother's declining health.

A metal bar above the bed in the back bedroom.

The pests living beneath the house.

And Jean always watching from across the way — her mother's eyes telling me she was her prisoner.

I went into the bathroom and closed the door, flipping the light switch on as sweat trickled down the back of my neck. I could swear Jean reflected in the mirror behind me. I even heard her voice yelling, I suppose, at me.

"Fever dream! Fever dream! Fever dream!" she yelled, laughing at me like some kid bantering on the playground. I eased my back toward the rear wall and sat down, working to separate my anxiety from my sleeplessness.

Jean chilled me — It must have been a demon hovering around her, some unknown heaviness in the air. And there I was, asking God in the troubling moment why He felt the need to burden me with a better read on her *this* way.

It would be unfair to tell Hannah. I wasn't going to ruin the excitement of our new beginning. A bit of research online told me new house anxiety was not uncommon. I was jarred by the reality of moving, but not for the reasons you'd think.

I studied the bathroom mirror a second too long, and I saw Jean in the reflection again. She took center stage, a microphone in hand, a red curtain behind, and the smoke and haze of something like a comedy club surrounding her.

*In my life to date, I've concluded tragedy and trauma are good for two things: shattering and rebuilding. That's not what's interesting. It's whether the pieces of you are ever put together the same after the first time you crack. You look yourself in the mirror and see your face. Every little piece of you glued back together after your breakdown. That voice inside you doing everything it can to take you down again as you glance at the inverse of yourself. You're not the same. And you never will be, but if you could package and sell an emotional glue like that, you'd make a fortune. Wouldn't ya? Ha-ha!*

The faceless audience applauded. I was jarred back to my senses, a dripping pool of sweat beneath. Climbing back into bed, I put my arm around Hannah. I needed reassurance that I wasn't alone.

# THERAPY

The parking lot was full for a Tuesday evening. Hannah and I stared up at the old church building. The years of decay and wear to its steeple showed, but it still stood — a beacon of hope for our troubled community. Most of the time, it wasn't the religion, but events like the ones we were there for.

It had been months since we'd been inside. It didn't feel any better now, even if it wasn't for Sunday service. It rained that night, the humidity was high, and emotions were raw.

A dead relative. Another failed statistic. Something to be blamed. It was rarely parents or education, the weight of the world, or predisposition to mental or physical ailments. The experts and idiots on TV always want it to be something material because that story sells better.

Maybe it's a video game.

A death metal band.

A medication.

A movie.

A hip new streaming series.

Constant recrimination's nothing more than a second-rate coping mechanism used to boost ratings.

We all have a part in humanity, giving life and taking it away. I suppose if you find a sort of peace in accepting that, it makes it easier to process a loss. I didn't think I was cold or calloused, but rather, trying to rationalize or reason through my struggles. That was all this was. I'd had my share of ups and downs.

As we pulled the doors open, we saw a clique of people standing on the far side, not laughing or smiling, but talking softly and hovering near a coffee pot. There were the usual religious things you'd expect: crosses, nails, thorns.

I looked at Hannah, picking up a brochure at the front of the building. Neither of us moved any closer to the others.

## GRIEF AND YOU

*Four out of five couples in situations of grief end up divorced in their first five years.*

I couldn't read anymore. It was disheartening. I loved Hannah. I wasn't disagreeing, but maybe there was a better way to package this. You know? Especially for someone in this position. Is it better to educate early? To normalize the stigma? It's unfair, the hand we were dealt. Somehow, I knew no matter how faithful or committed we might be, it wasn't personal. This was no punishment of God. It was science. If you got exposed to an illness, took in too much of anything toxic, or ended up sicker than normal, you were at a higher risk, and often, you didn't get the seventy-eight years you expected. It's always the miserable ones that live to a hundred while the rest of us end up dead of a stroke or heart attack by sixty. I suppose it all comes full circle in pursuit of eternity. That's what I hope for, anyway.

As the clock struck seven, I put the brochure back in the container storing a dozen others just like it. Hannah and I found our way toward the group. We sat in a grief circle with others. Some were missing wedding bands. Others had tear-soaked eyes. Our counselor looked and smelled barely sober, if I'm honest with you. This wasn't AA. It was Grief Support. In this circle, they offered no judgment, only encouragement and trust. People coped in their own ways, and that was understandable.

Even better, they rarely discouraged us from drowning ourselves in distractions. In a modern context like this, these things were all part of the logical path to healing. It was a bunch of bunk, if you asked me, but it was better that I kept a positive attitude. We were walking through a valley of struggle on a journey to find our way again. That's where we were.

I heard little of what anyone said that night. A middle-aged lady with pathetic red-hair dye started the group, sharing about how she lost her son in a car accident five years before, and how that was the start of an unending depression. The only thing I took from her monologue was that she gets her Pomeranian's tail teased every other Thursday and when I got to thinking about the bills racking up on such a trivial thing, I got wound up. The next one said something about their little grandson, that they'd forgotten to lock the gate to the swimming pool. It riddled them with guilt, knowing that was the end of the line. To add to the family drama, they went on to admit they never talked with their son again because he never forgave them. Awful story, and my sincere condolences, but I struggled to fathom if this group was helpful for us. It hadn't been long enough. I lost touch again.

Oh, the game of life. It's full of chance and opportunity and tragedy and so on and so forth.

Blah. Blah. Blah.

So, I'm sitting there in the circle doing what most neurotics of my sort would do. My internal monologue running over and over about what I would say, how I would say it, and why. I think it's a normal sort of speaking anxiety, my heartbeat palpitating as we went around the room, sharing losses and little tidbits about ourselves. The therapist said it was about vulnerability and honesty. The brochure did, too. And the most disheartening thing about it was that most people in the circle were still dishonest. I could read them. It wasn't telepathy, just observation — body language, eye contact, posture, breath rhythms, that kind of stuff.

I stood in a wilderness of suffering trying to lead a crumbling family running from a mania I didn't understand. Before it was my turn, a balding man in his upper forties talked about losing his wife nine months earlier to something called CSD, and a little while before that, how they'd lost their teenage son. My eyes were stuck on the reflection in the middle of his forehead, the fluorescent light hitting it. Somehow, I could swear he shined his head every night to get that nice sheen.

I'd never heard of CSD, so later that night I looked it up, and nothing seemed to match this guy's descriptions.

Cold shock domain.

Charlie Sheen Derangement.

A cause specified death.

Or maybe it was a carotid sinus denervation.

My personal favorite, cat scratch disease. Now, that would be a cat-astrophe. If you died that way, maybe you were meant to cross over early. Or God decided cats would go to heaven, and you'd be the gatekeeper. Lucky you!

I gave up. Maybe I'd figure it out, or perhaps it was insignificant. The man stood out. All these sob stories were real downers, and I wondered if this kind of therapy would take us into the pits with more questions than answers. When death sucks the color from your life, there's no getting it back. It just fades to black for a while and comes back slowly in shades of gray.

I jibber-jabbered something to the group and Hannah followed. The smiles, tears, and head nods told us we were welcomed into the fold. I suppose that was a good thing. I couldn't accept it, though. It felt insincere. I didn't think people had much to hide in these settings. It was more about the sort of white lies told on a whim that bothered me.

As the group ended, we grabbed our folding chairs and hung them up on a stacking cart with wheels. Picking up a few extras, I did the same for the older guests as a courtesy. I looked at the therapist and smiled. My behavior was unnatural, but I was there, right?

"I'm glad you're here," the therapist said. "It's not an easy step, but accountability in this process is pivotal to acceptance."

I nodded and looked over at Hannah. "Yeah..." I said, with a bit of a sniffle. "It's... uh... probably in everyone's best interest we are."

I was reluctant to be truly present (my scarlet letter of a sin), but I knew it meant something to Hannah. I wanted to do what I could to move the cloud hovering above in whatever way I could. It may not have been only my burden to carry, but there were none closer to the middle of it than I was. Seventy-two steps to the car, a bit of light rain, and some soft jazz on the radio. It was something to squash the silence without words.

As we neared our destination, I found myself lost in the thick of emotions, perhaps not visibly, but internally. The surroundings changed as we crossed town to the east side. I looked at Hannah.

"What did you think?"

"It was about what I expected," she said.

"Same. Do you want to go back?"

"I don't know if 'want' is the right word, but I see value in it, yeah."

I nodded. "That seems fair. Maybe not forever, but for a while."

We pulled into Hal's driveway.

My mind wandered to Dad. When I was eleven, he'd park behind the fence at the baseball fields and watch me from the car, his cigarettes queued up. He'd even have one tucked over his right ear for moments when he was on the move. A cooler sat behind the passenger seat under a blanket where a six-pack remained an arm's length away.

I'd strike out and look out there. His expressions were animated. He'd grab at his throat, throw his hands in the air, or yell phrases like, "Come on!" and all the coaches and other kids would hear it and look at me. I always imagined him cheering, that stamp of approval I longed for but never received.

"Are you gonna get him or not?" Hannah asked, bringing me back to the moment.

"Oh, yeah. Sorry. I was lost in my own little world."

"Welcome back," she said, giving me two pats on the shoulder. Something told me she knew I was defective.

# GRUNT WORK

I'd be remiss if I didn't admit things had gotten strange since the divestiture, but they were improving. I pulled into the company lot, checking my hair in the vanity mirror. My days in the office were slower, but I had to catch up on the paperwork when I wasn't in the field selling.

I was in a weird mood, but I was no Willy Loman. The sales strategy had me answering more for big picture goals than direct sales, but I loved proving I was an asset, often outselling those in my reporting lines.

Historically, these days were all about catching up on work and whatever else I felt like. Plenty to do, but at a leisurely pace, my leisurely pace. This was the Ben Decker way, and though it may have been unpopular amongst the former management chain, the tables were reset again, and the timing couldn't be more impeccable.

I loosened my necktie a bit from the collar. It was a white shirt, black tie day like every other Monday. I'd adjusted to the company's jeans casual policy with a pair of Justin boots but never ditched the tie. That tie was my trademark. It made me look more important than I was. As for the rest of me, I cut corners frequently.

Unshaven.

Horn-rimmed glasses, not contacts.

My hair perfectly parted with mousse.

I preferred the routine.

Predictability's key to establishing comfort zone. Real life loves to disrupt that, so when you find your way into the same parking spot or the same pair of socks on a certain day, you find yourself more at home, even when you aren't.

I wrapped the afternoon up — filing away another day to be forgotten. The day's events left me with no takeaways beyond the reminder I was burned out. Though we had all these changes at the top of the organization, keeping my job wasn't enough to satisfy.

My mind drifted.

I was working late on the east side to close some deals. Hannah had gone to bed and then woken in a panic. I arrived home to the police lights. Peeking through the window, Hannah's feverish maneuvers and the compulsive running of her fingertips through her hair told me something was very wrong. I walked into the house in what felt a perpetual slow motion. Our eyes met, and I knew she'd cracked, certainly more than I had at that point. It was the tone in her voice as she spoke with the policeman. "I don't know, officer. He didn't come home from school."

Davey was asleep in his room.

"Honey, what's going on?" I asked, looking at her a moment and then toward the officer.

She clung to a photograph we'd taken the previous Christmas. "It's Jake. He never came home today."

I shook my head. No part of me wanted to be cold, but I had to be real. "He can't. Remember?"

She teared up, her cries becoming uncontrollable.

"What do you mean? What are you saying?" the officer asked.

"Our ten-year-old, Jake, we lost him about a month and a half ago."

Hannah screamed.

I came closer, wrapping my arms around her.

Davey hugged us both. "What's wrong, Mommy?" he asked.

"Can we turn the flashing lights off, please?" I asked. "We're making a scene here."

The officer nodded. "I'm really sorry. Ma'am, sir, if there's anything you need, any help, a grief counselor, anything at all..."

# MOVING DAY

The roll-top door on the moving truck slid up.

The fruits of your materialism showcased for the world to see. So many branded items from the Crate and Barrel, the Pottery Barn, and beyond. Things you collected through the years, some hand-me-downs, some ordered from catalogs, and others curated and brought straight home on discount from a showroom floor. You keep up appearances. You want to do what you can to fit in with the circles you walk in. I guess that's the reason for the Mercedes and Range Rover. They're niceties with hefty price tags when you need specialized repairs, but that satisfaction every time someone sees you driving it, either envious or spewing with excitement — that's a little contagious.

As the truck's contents thinned out, we waved workers in and around our new home, directing them to drop zones for furniture and boxes. Breathless and dehydrating in the August heat, two men took a seat on our wraparound porch. Davey pumped his legs on the wood block swing draped from the large live oak standing tall and healthy in the front yard.

Our new place was magazine ready. An old-fashioned southern charmer with nice Crape Myrtle trees, hedged landscaping, a porch swing, and every amenity most would hope for. Sitting on the east side of the home, Hannah and I faced the stop sign near Avenue J and 17th in a set of matching white rockers delivered early at her request. If we avoided looking west, 1739 remained inconsequential. This didn't mean we could avoid it, though. One thing our previous home taught me through the years, curb appeal remains a priority for appraisals and taxes.

I studied the adjacent streets and homes up and down.

"I think this might just be the most beautiful place in town," I said, resting my hand above Hannah's knee. She was wearing a navy dress that day, a sun hat, and sunglasses, and I couldn't be more attracted.

She dropped her hand on top of mine and bit her lip for a second. "Hey! You did great picking it out."

"Thanks for that, milady."

"I'm so glad we're finally here," she said. "We only live once... might as well make it count."

I smiled and rubbed my chin. "Yeah. A new school year for Davey, a new everything for us, a fresh start. No more extended stays in the rear-view. Deal?"

"Deal," she said.

As the day went on, we directed workers into each room of our home, finally giving the place a chance to breathe again.

"When did you say this was built?" Hannah asked.

"1924," I said. "It's a year from historic landmark status. Thank God."

She studied me and laughed. "What are you thanking God for?"

I sighed, rubbing my forehead, my voice becoming softer. "It's a lot of extra upkeep. You know, a sign in the yard, blah, blah, blah. Just because we can afford it doesn't mean we should."

Hannah shook her head and snickered. "Usually, I'm the tightwad. We can swing this, can't we, Ben?"

"Of course," I said, gawking at the question. "You know I'm willing to splurge, but there are limits."

"Such as?"

"I don't know... paying for historical landmark upkeep, excess throw pillows, three-hundred-dollar blue jeans, all that crap."

She chuckled. "Speaking of excess."

A large Mercedes pulled up out front, four years newer than mine, and double the *Blue Book* value. The bright red color stood out against the monochrome block of houses lining the neighboring streets.

I squinted a second, studying the vehicle. "Oh, that's Mori. What's he doing here?"

"He already knows our address?" she asked. "You don't have to make every detail of our life a public service announcement first thing, do you?"

I scoffed, my blood pressure rising. "Yeah... I told him about it the other day. You know, water cooler chit-chat."

"Well, I would have preferred him to wait for a housewarming party, not our moving day."

Mori jumped out and waved. He approached the porch, studied the movers, and nodded and clapped. "Stunning, Ben. Wow! Such classic craftsmanship," he said, reaching out his hand to shake mine, and leaning in to give an extended bear hug. He handed me a paper sack tied up in a red bow. "I brought you little warmhousing gift. You know, new to neighborhood? It's good. I think you like it."

"Oh, thanks, Mori. You didn't have to do that," I said, taking the sack. "This is my wife, Hannah."

"Nice to meet you... Beautiful. You must be from mother country, too. Yeah? You know your roots, huh?"

She shook her head.

The question seemed misplaced. Mori was, too. This was our moment, not his.

"I don't know," she said. "I think I have some eastern European in me on my father's side, but mom was German."

"Very good," he said, looking back at me. "Your son... so nice to see him enjoy beautiful yard. You should put pictures of family on desk. I like when workers touch personal."

I looked at Mori. "Personal touch. When they add a personal touch."

"Right, hmm-hmm," he said, chuckling with his teeth gritted.

Hannah opened the sack, pulling out a bottle of fancy wine and Gouda cheese.

"Oh, Mori. This is too much. Thanks," she said.

He grabbed her by the arm and kissed her cheek. "My pleasure, dorogáya."

Hannah blushed.

Mori's grin was huge, the kindest of faces. "We get you guys settled in well. Let Olkov take care of you. Yes. Yes. Ben's team... busy selling cycle coming soon. Will help commissions. I won't take more time," he said, dismissing himself, waving at Davey, and walking away.

"Goodbye, Mori," I said.

"Welcome home!"

As Mori got back in the car, his stereo grew louder.

Hannah looked at me and smiled. "Is that *NSYNC? He really is charming!"

I nodded. "Yeah. Typical Mori. Nice gift."

"Too nice," she said, stroking her fingers through my hair. I caught her in the reflection of the window behind us, studying my scalp closer, questioning what was left of my natural hairline compared to the one purchased with last year's Christmas bonus. My hair plugs were holding up well, and they made me look more like twenty-six than the thirty-six I was — a perfect U shape, not too flat across the front, a very natural job.

"It's still there, hun," I said.

She chuckled. "And no longer financed."

"Four thousand grafts later..." I said, sighing, as a truck drove by faster than the posted speed limit. "People have kids here!" I yelled, standing up, and throwing my hands in the air. "How about some cheese and wine? Mori rarely does things on the cheap."

"Alright. That works for me," she said, moving toward the front door, cool beads of sweat running down the back of her neck. "Time for some air conditioning... the mosquitos are awful."

We motioned to Davey to come inside, maneuvering him toward the backyard.

As the sun set for the evening, the workers finished up and prepped to leave as I signed off on the work order form and tipped them more generously than they deserved.

"Thanks for your help today. You guys were a professional crew. Appreciate you not swearing every other word around my kid. I get sick of that. Make it count when you cuss. You know?"

"Ha! Of course, Mr. Decker. It's our pleasure. I hope you find happy memories in your home. Have a damn good night," the lead mover said.

I laughed. "I'm sure we will."

Hannah's efforts at hospitality kicked in late. "Did you guys want any lemonade before you go? I whipped up a fresh batch."

"No, ma'am," the mover replied. "We better get on our way."

***

My study was attached to the patio, separate from the house and parallel to the backyard, giving autonomy from excess pop-ins. It was an ideal place to focus, escape, and catch up on work.

Hannah knocked on the door and I laid my phone on the desk. "What are you doing?" she asked, coming in playfully, wrapping her arm around my neck. "Are you 'working' again? I thought you took a vacation day."

Her sweet smile was wide and renewed, clearly riding a high from our arrival to the new place. I wanted to bottle the moment up and hold on to it. The realist in me told me it wouldn't be this great forever.

I rocked in the swiveling chair in my study and sighed, sliding my phone in my pocket. The chair was one of the few furniture pieces properly placed from the get-go. "You know there's no such thing in sales, honey. Stay nimble to stay ahead."

"Alright. I'm gonna start making heads or tails of what's in our room. I can't stand the clutter. Our clothes won't find their way into the dresser or closet on their own."

I pursed my lips a moment. "If you want to, that's fine. Or, if you want to take it easy tonight, that's fine too. I can get us a housekeeper if you want to delegate some of that to her."

"To her, huh? 'Just because we can afford it doesn't mean we should,'" she said, imitating my voice.

I rolled my eyes. "I thought you'd appreciate some extra help. I know... Davey keeps us plenty busy."

"No. I'd prefer to go through *your* unmentionables on my own," she said. "And I don't need some nosy housekeeper meddling around or knowing I'm a C cup."

I laughed. "I don't think it takes a rocket scientist to figure that out. If you want to fold your own clothes, be my guest. If you don't, whatever. I just want to give you the time and creative space to do more things you enjoy and less rigorous day-to-day stuff you don't want to be stuck with.

She nodded. "Thanks, Ben. Everyone can pitch in, you know. It doesn't have to all be me."

I smiled. "Yes, that's true, but life with a silver spoon comes with benefits. We've earned it!" I said, walking out of my study and back inside to the main living area. I plopped on the couch, flipping on the TV. Stallone was busy arm wrestling.

Hannah was a few steps behind. "You've got it made, don't you, Ben Decker?" she called from across the room, motioning her head toward a bunch of boxes to unload.

"Couch, cable, and TV — Man's best friends."

"A lot of help you are," she said, rolling her eyes.

"If this was *Rhinestone*, you'd have sat down in a heartbeat."

She hurled a throw pillow at me.

"Remind me why we have so many of these again?"

"Seasonal decorations!"

The sunset shined through the long row of our west windows, but the shadow of 1739 blocked a portion of it.

"When are we getting the drapes hung?" I asked. "A little privacy goes a long way, you know? And then we don't have to look at... that."

She nodded. "First thing tomorrow."

"I'm gonna order us a pizza," I said. "Any beer in the fridge?"

"Sure, *Norm*... we've got plenty. After the cheese and wine from Mori, you want beer and pizza? What is this... a frat house?"

"Yep!" I said, an over-pronounced P at the end. I dug my hand into a bowl of honey roasted peanuts, lobbing them into my mouth.

"You can figure that out on your own," she said, a little tipsy.

I muted the TV. "You want something else or what?"

"No. Pizza sounds good."

The movie cut to a commercial break and I spaced-out, drifting into an afternoon daze.

Jean's voice raced through my mind at a rapid spitfire rhythm.

*It's smart to get to work on time. I do it often. And sometimes, I don't. Just because the little voice in my head tells me to ruffle a feather, you know, to make a manager sweat. If you get a goody two-shoes three-hundred-sixty-five days a year less the two weeks of vacation, you're not real. You're nothing but a machine. A sick and twisted little lie waiting to be unwound at the right moment and exposed like the two-timing executive you are! I'd rather be real, raw, and calculated. If I accept the truth that people trust me with too much, I get my way, jabbing my proverbial knife right where it needs to go and when. Dangerous, I know. Danger is, you see, what you make of it. And what I make of it. And what we make of it. The craziest part, we're all wrapped around each other's fingers even when we don't want to be. Creatures longing for compatibility and swimming in the same dark sea, predators abounding. I won't be a victim again. I'm doing it my way.*

And then, as quickly as she came into my head, she stopped, and I felt not an anxiety, but a therapeutic peace — that even though she intruded my thoughts, she was gone again.

The TV remained on a commercial break. I stood up, still unsettled.

Hannah emerged from our bedroom. I walked toward her, hugging her, the warmth of our bodies interlocking and reminding me of our most cherished moments. As much as I thought she experienced the same, we remained on different wavelengths.

"Hey, Dad..." she said. "Why don't you go outside and check on your son? You can do that, can't you?"

"Yeah, yeah," I said, deflecting. "I'll go out there and check on him in a minute. He's big enough not to want me around all the time, you know? Let's enjoy a quiet, air-conditioned minute to ourselves."

"Quiet? That TV's been too loud to call anything quiet. It must be nice not to be bothered."

I smiled. "Step back a little and give him some space. Let him skin his knee. Climb a tree. Sneak an extra popsicle. They're only kids once. It's not the worst thing in the world for a mother to loosen up, is it? God knows you know that."

It was a careless comment. I studied her for a second, recognizing my gaffe. "I love you, sweetheart. You're an exceptional mother to that kid."

My default smooth-over routine fell miserably flat.

*Nice going, Ben.*

"I love you," she said sarcastically, her eyes wandering away. "Pizza here soon?"

"Yep."

# FRIENDS AND ENEMIES

It was another Tuesday night at home last fall. We cooked little, but ate plenty, sadly remaining on a first name basis with every takeout driver in town. Hannah prepped a few plates and set the table while Davey poured ice into our glasses. Jake had just come in from cutting the grass in our backyard and rinsed in the shower.

Our 1970s era tract home was well-dressed and maintained, but the place rarely lent itself to anything I'd call photogenic. It was a house, but never a home.

The doorbell rang. I peeked out the window and noticed the Chow Fung's truck had arrived out front. I answered the door, grabbing the food and tipping the takeout driver.

"Yeah, thanks a lot."

The man bowed, nodding his head toward me. "Our pleasure, Mr. Decker. We hope you enjoy the Lo-Mein tonight."

"We sure will. Thanks," I said, closing the door.

I brought the sack over and dropped it on the kitchen table, smiling at Hannah. Jake came out of the bathroom, his hair still wet.

Davey ran to the back door and looked out at the lawn. "It looks great, Jake! Nice job!"

"Appreciate you, guy," I said, trusting Davey's assessment.

In all reality, Jake was still learning, and I was having to touch it up afterwards to keep Hannah appeased, but we did what we could to minimize it, appreciating his well-mannered contributions to our family — our perfect little family of four. Davey carried a jug of store-bought iced tea to the table. We bowed our heads a moment and then the typical clank of plates and Decker household banter began.

I sat down. My seat faced the west window, next to Jake's, while Hannah and Davey were side by side, just across.

"How was your day, buddy?" I asked, looking toward Davey — the spitting image of his mother with shorter hair.

"It was okay, dad. The teacher in social studies was telling us about friends and enemies."

"Friends and enemies, huh?"

"Yeah. Like how to tell them apart."

"And what did she say?"

"She said, 'friends are there for each other no matter what. No strings attached.'"

"And enemies?"

"She said, 'enemies look the same, but they look out for their own good... There are strings attached.'"

"Not a bad description for a first grader," Hannah said, looking at me and raising her eyebrows as if to tell me not to over-talk the subject. I guess I ignored the cue.

"That's one of life's most important lessons," I replied. "Even most grown-ups struggle with that."

"What does 'strings attached' mean?" Davey asked, raking some rice into his mouth while another clump dropped onto the table.

"I guess it just means that when you do something nice for someone, you expect them to do something in return, to sort of pay you back."

"But if a friend comes with no strings attached, you wouldn't need to pay them back, would you?" Jake asked.

I don't think our boys got their smarts from me. Hannah carried the brain power in our family. I was just neurotic.

"Yeah, I guess you could say that," Hannah said. "Good friends don't expect it."

"But enemies do?" Davey asked.

"Why bother if they're an enemy?" Jake said, inserting himself again.

"Sometimes you don't have a choice," I replied. "I guess it's a matter of... forced proximity."

"What do you mean, *Dad*?" Hannah asked, smirking as she sipped her tea.

"Sometimes people we're not ready for come into our life and you can't always push them away if you don't get along. New coworkers, in-laws, IRS auditors, baristas, Russians..."

"Ben!" Hannah said, kicking me in the shin.

"But why are they your enemy?" Davey asked, finishing his rice.

"Well, there are people that fit somewhere in between. We'll call them acquaintances, professional connections, colleagues."

The crinkle of the wrapper caught my attention as Davey worked to pry a fortune cookie from it.

"Well... what's it say? What do our Chinese friends have to enlighten us with?" I asked, looking at Davey.

He studied it for a second and handed it to Jake. "What does it mean?"

Jake read it slowly. *"The best lies are told somewhere between home and work, and yet, somehow, they bleed together, forever meant to be."*

"Not inaccurate," I said, reaching out to hold Hannah's hand.

"Hmm," Davey said, sipping the last of his tea through a straw. "Well?"

I looked toward Hannah, hoping she'd bail me out. "It means..."

"You don't always get to leave your work at work," she said.

"Why lies? Do you lie at work, Daddy?"

"I guess everyone does a little, bud."

"But we shouldn't lie, should we, Mom?"

Hannah shook her head. "We shouldn't, but we do."

She grinned at me and furled her lip.

"What's new in your world, Momma?" I asked, looking at Hannah.

"Not much."

"Why do you say that?" I asked, taking a bite of the Lo-Mein.

"I eat my lunch alone, wash dishes, and fold clothes. You guys wear me out. Thirty-four's not the same as twenty-four. You're ready for bed earlier."

"This is the perfect object lesson," I said, patting Hannah on the hand across the table. "Davey's learning about friends and enemies and it sounds like we need to make a friend. What should we do?"

"I don't know, Daddy."

"Of course you do, bud. Friends find their way like seasons," I said. "Your mom and I have been stretched thin lately. We haven't made a lot of time to socialize."

For a split second, my eyes locked on the kitchen window. I looked over at Hannah and then got up and washed my hands at the sink. I wanted to make sure things were okay. It was just a squirrel on the air conditioning unit outside.

"Everything alright?" Jake asked.

"Yep. All good."

"If your dad gets that promotion we're hoping for, things will change soon," Hannah said.

I walked back to the table and sat down. "You bet! I love you guys."

Hannah looked at me. "And?"

"You gal."

She smiled, giving me a look that told me our evening would be memorable.

# WARM APPLE PIE

Hannah and I reclined on our sectional, still in a dreamlike state, as we admired our new home. The lights were dimmed a few notches as evening overtook the afternoon. I'd promised a few uninterrupted minutes away from my phone and the TV and any other looming commitments. I was certain this spoke volumes to Hannah, considering her warmth.

"This place really is perfect. I don't know what else to say, but I love it!" she said, taking me by the hand. A rush of jubilation coursed through me.

"Right place, right time. That's all this was," I said, leaning toward her and kissing her on the cheek.

"Davey loves it, too. That playset in the backyard is great."

I nodded, glancing across the room, studying the fireplace that took center stage — its bricked column stretching from floor to ceiling, fully exposed and shaped.

"Yeah. I thought the playset was a nice touch. We lost some square footage, but we gained a better backyard and a real garage. And that back patio. We're gonna love it."

Hannah smiled. As Davey played out back, I got up and poured some aged Chardonnay from the bottle Mori gave us into a matching set of chilled glasses and approached, placing the wine on our drink coasters.

"To our new life," I said, raising my glass and clinking it with Hannah's.

"To new beginnings," she said, sipping and leaning in to kiss me.

We fell onto the couch, our arms wrapping around one another in a tight embrace — a potential warmup for later — and then the back door flew open before it slammed. Davey was crying. And there went whatever good thing was happening between Hannah and me. We were used to it. It's just something parents with kids adjust to. As selfish as it sounds, you don't realize how much you appreciate those moments until you're in a state of perpetual interruption. It's part of the job description.

Hannah jumped up, wiping the wine from her lips, as she scurried toward him. She was cute in nurturing mother mode.

"What's wrong?"

"I fell off the fence."

I stood up, my defense mechanisms kicking in, more frustrated with Davey about the interruption to our tender moment than carrying sympathy. "Why'd you do that? Are you okay?"

Dabbing the tears from his eyes, Davey's trembling voice stabilized. "I don't know. I guess I just lost my balance. I was curious."

He sniffled, over and over, in line with the pattern. There's a certain tone in a child's cry, in their voice, that a parent comes to know. You figure out when they're hurt and when they're putting on an act. Davey wasn't acting, but to say he wasn't hamming it up with some extra theatrics to get Mommy's undivided attention would be unfair, because he was. Though, we all knew, we enabled it.

Hannah kissed him on the forehead, "It'll be okay, buddy."

"There's a hole looking in the neighbor's backyard. It's full of junk. Old cars, barb-wire fences, and a gigantic pile of dog shit with flies all over it."

Hannah raised her finger over her lips. "Watch your mouth. You know you don't like to eat soap."

"I heard Daddy say it the other day when he dropped that box on his toe."

"Is that right?" Hannah asked, looking back and grinning at me. "Well, I guess Daddy gets some soap in his mouth, too."

I should have been more playful. I grabbed Davey by the shoulder firmly. "Look at me. We don't spy on people. We mind our business, and they should mind theirs. You understand?"

"I don't want to," he said, turning around and running back outside, the tears stopping on cue. I was ready to follow him out and hand more to him. Disrespect never sat well with me, nor my old man.

"Ben," Hannah said, a tone in her voice, "go easy on him. He's six. Let him discover... wander and find piles of dog... stuff."

"I know. I know. I think I'm just a little tense about the new locale. It shortens my fuse, you know? With all these new neighbors, we should just welcome each other at a comfortable pace, never any faster. I'm sure this is an adjustment to them as much as it is to us, and maybe we aren't mindful enough of how our life disrupts theirs."

"That's actually kind of thoughtful, Ben," she said, patting me on the shoulder. "Good save."

She peeked into the back bedroom, where an easel and a row of blank canvases leaned against the wall, with stacks and boxes of Jake's things scattered in various corners.

"It'll be good to see you in action in there. I'm looking forward to the new things you paint. This place should offer you plenty of inspiration."

"I know it will," she said.

Before I could go out back to check on Davey, there was a tap at the front door.

"Ben, would you get that?"

We made eye contact, and I sighed, reluctantly walking toward the front of the house. I did my share of socializing for work. Somewhere within me, I always hoped the neighborly stuff would be hers. I checked the peephole on the front door.

"It's Jean, she's holding... a pie," I said, looking back at Hannah.

I opened the door and greeted her. It was only our second encounter, but I felt I knew her better than I did especially after the intrusive run-ins we'd had in my head.

Hannah peeked around the corner of the kitchen as she poured a couple of glasses of lemonade, perhaps to choke the stench of the wine from our breaths. "Great!"

"Welcome to the neighborhood!" Jean said, her smile oversized, her voice chipper, and much brighter than before. Her black dress and earrings caught my attention. Everyone's entitled to a private moment to themselves, to walk around in their favorite dingy sweatpants and shirt with holes in it. This was a remarkable transformation, though. For a quick moment, it opened me up to the idea that Jean was more normal than I surmised, and I was one step from certifiably insane.

First impressions make all the difference, because that's how people remember you. As we made eye contact, I noticed some blush on her cheeks, her gray-blue eyes accentuated by eyeliner. The tone in my voice got deeper and more pronounced, whether I admitted it or not. "Thank you. Wow! It smells fantastic," I said, collecting the pie and grinning.

"It's my pleasure," she said, her laugh a little nervous. Her voice seemed a tad more Southern belle than the first time we'd met, too. I could've sworn she had the upper Midwestern nasal thing going before, but then again, what did I know?

"Remind me your name again, darlin'?"

"Ben. Ben Decker," I said, reaching out to shake her hand as Hannah collected the pie.

"That's right... Benjamin," she said, adjusting her pearl beaded necklace and smiling at me.

"Have a seat, Jean," Hannah said, pulling out a chair from our elongated kitchen table. The living room opened into the dining area, making for a nice space to visit and socialize through and through.

"I don't want to intrude, y'all," she said, walking back toward the door. "But wow, this is really nice now. You guys have upped the ante around here. Kind of classed up the block, didn't ya?"

"Why don't you stay for a glass of wine?" I asked.

Hannah glared at me, telling me to tone the friendliness down. She helped keep me in check.

Jean blushed. "Well, that's sweet, but I've got to head on to work. Got to pay the bills, you know?" she said, stepping back toward the door.

"Fair enough. What line of work are you in? We didn't get to talk about it the other day," I asked.

Her reply was curt as she reached for the doorknob. "That's personal."

"Oh, I'm sorry. I... didn't mean to intrude. Just boilerplate conversation starters, right?" I said, looking back at Hannah.

Jean waved me off, a grin coming across her face, a flirtatious tone in her voice. "Boilerplate?"

"Yes."

"You are some kind of businessman, aren't you?" she asked, her eagerness to leave slowing. It was a subtle change in her posture. "I just... I don't even know what you guys do yet. Ha-ha. I figure it's polite to let you do the talking first, with ya being new and all. Ya know?"

"Don't let us hold you up, Jean," Hannah said abruptly.

"I guess I've got another minute or two," she said.

I caught Jean looking around the room, observing all the quirky things of ours that had not yet found a proper place. Outside of a few steins on the mantel and some eclectic costume jewelry of Hannah's strewn on the counter, there was little to notice. No photographs or knick-knacks yet, just boxes lining the living room wall with poor penmanship and box tape bunched up in all the wrong places, most of which was my doing.

"Well, Jean, I'm in pharmaceutical sales. It keeps me on the road a lot more than I'd like it to. I practically live out of my car, but at least it's all regional these days."

She looked at Hannah. "That explains the nice wheels you've got. And you, darlin'?"

"I stay home. Davey keeps me plenty busy."

Jean sighed, puffing air through her nose. "And in your spare time?"

"Spare time... What's that again?"

I had no way of diffusing cattiness between women, but I knew everything about bearing witness to it. I looked at Hannah, my eyes widening, and back at Jean. I gave it my best. "Hannah helps keep this place organized and my head on straight. My job's high pressure, and since I don't have an assistant, she manages most of my affairs."

"Your... affairs?" Jean asked, a gulp in her throat.

"Yeah. She handles my appointments, manages my calendar, all that good stuff. We make a great team."

"Well, that's good to hear. I better get to it," she said. "Don't want to be late. It's a Dutch apple pie, by the way." Her gaze lingered in my direction.

"Thanks," Hannah said, her voice tense. "Have a good evening. We'll get the pan back to you soon. The warm welcome means a lot."

"No need," Jean said, letting herself out the front door. "It's my gift. We'll do coffee together soon, darlin'. Do mornings work well for you?"

"That sounds good," Hannah said.

She walked back toward her house, starting her vehicle in the driveway before going inside.

"Hmm, that was kind of weird," I said.

"What? The way she was talking? She sure talked sweet with you, didn't she?"

"Yeah. I noticed that, too. I'll keep a healthy distance, and you probably should, too, but that's not what I meant. Why did she dodge the question about her job?"

Hannah shook her head. "That didn't seem to stop you, Mister Charmer. 'Why don't you stay for a glass of wine?'" she said, mockingly.

"Too much?"

"Oh yeah, Ben."

"I think we've got to be careful around her." Glancing out the window, her kitchen curtains closed abruptly, and the lights went out. She walked out to the Roadmaster, driving away in a hurry. Its backfire was quick to follow.

"What do you mean?"

I had more to say but wasn't sure how. "Didn't she have a limp the first time we met?"

"Yeah. I bet she was just having a rough day. Overdid it with the weed eater or something."

"Weed eating? You saw the yard, right?" I asked. "The pie smells good. You think I should give it a good once-over. Just in case she's a little...?" I whistled and rotated my finger in circles next to my head.

"I think we're all a little..." Hannah said, whistling and repeating the sound and motion. "It's just nature."

"Sometimes, it's nurture," I said.

"She's just trying to help us settle in."

"Then maybe she shouldn't be so... unsettling."

"People are fragile," she said. "Sometimes, that makes them unpredictable. She's divorced, remember? From the look in her eyes the other day, it's still recent. I bet it's raw."

"Yeah. Besides, if she did try to poison us, she'd be smart enough not to waste so many good apples. Now if it were a lemon pie..."

Hannah chuckled. "You're a strange man, Ben Decker, and probably right."

I stepped into the backyard and called for Davey. The lush St. Augustine grass was soft and I'm sure his bare feet were taking it for granted. It was a luxury our other place never had, no matter how many times I tried. I peered at the adjacent storage building and detached garage, envisioning many projects and our family's future. No mutts to ruin the soil, a perfect amount of shade to squash the heat, and nice privacy fences adding further security to our activities. I spotted the holed notch Davey had been spying through on the fence facing west. Sure enough, abandoned cars, barbed wire, and well-aged... dog stuff. I didn't see much else worthy of mention, but it would take a lot to get *that* backyard in any kind of order.

"Time to come in, partner," I said, calling toward Davey.

"Why? I don't want to," he replied.

"But there's a treat!"

"What treat?"

"Miss Jean brought us an apple pie, and we picked up some vanilla bean ice cream from the store earlier."

He hopped down from the playset making a beeline toward the back door.

"Tell your mom I'll be inside in just a second."

I went toward the garage, pulling out a tube of caulk left over from the home's renovations. I didn't have my tools organized, but I knew which box had which tool, and that was enough for the moment. That would work for a good long while as busy as I stayed. I'd get around to it when I felt like it and keep it locked up the rest of the time. Caulk wasn't the best choice, but it was a start. I approached the fence, filling in the hole and doing a quick walk around the property, closing other questionable spots, and checking the structural integrity of each board. Hannah checked on me through the back window a couple of times, but never bothered to interrupt. The new house excitement was plenty to keep us amused. My second-rate caulk job clashed with the weathered wood, but it worked for what we needed it for and, perhaps, would deter Davey from excessive spying.

Caulking the holes in the fence, I drifted.

I arrived home from work that evening. Hannah and Davey were at the table, sharing a pizza. Our oldest, Jake, was in the back bedroom recovering from a fever-stricken bout with the flu. I kissed and greeted Hannah unceremoniously, still coming down from the little blue pill, and doing what I could to act normal, which in and of itself was difficult. Stepping into our bedroom, I dropped my work bag next to the bed and washed my hands for our evening meal. I checked the mirror, fixed my hair, and took a few deep breaths. I didn't expect them to wait but was thankful when we could intersect and catch up. These kinds of moments, regardless of how much conversation we did or didn't have, were special and I never took them for granted, not intentionally, anyway.

I sat down. We were a blessed family with every reason in the world to smile, even in moments where stress invited itself in without our permission.

"Still got one missing in action, huh?" I asked.

Hannah nodded. "Yeah. He was at 101.2, last I checked. I gave him some aspirin to bring the fever down. That was all we had left, though. Can you get some from the store tonight after we get Davey tucked in?"

I sighed. "It's been four days. He'll be on the mend before we know it. Let the fever fight for a while."

"Why do you have to do this, Ben?"

"Do what?"

"Get difficult when you don't have to?"

"I don't know. I'm just exhausted."

Her eyes told me she'd had a sleepless night. To make matters worse, I was dumb enough to take my first dose of Garashock 500 an hour before I left the office, so while I was in a daze of my own, my ten-year-old was sick and my wife was a walking zombie, we also had another kid desperate for attention, which neither of us could truly give.

"I wish you would just go," she said. "We don't have to give any to him, but we could at least have some on hand in case it gets worse overnight."

It must have been the pill talking because I was a jerk that night. When it's time to find the path of least resistance, inevitably, I drift the other way. Her tone had jarred me. "Can't you drive? You should have planned better," I said. "This divestiture with Olkov has me beat. I can't make heads or tails with this Mori guy and it's wearing me out."

Her cold stare told me I was better off dead. Somehow, she shoved her feelings away, but we both knew it was an act for Davey, enabling my selfishness momentarily, to punish me later when the timing was right. I certainly deserved a good tongue-lashing. I'll admit that.

"Yeah. I'll go later, then," she said.

*Then*. It was always that extra word at the end that told me I was in trouble. That passive aggressive qualifier meant I was headed for the couch, but the little blue pill I'd taken had a voice of its own, instructing me to hold my ground rather than yield like she hoped for me to do. I wouldn't compromise on the matter.

After a few bites of cold pizza and an uncomfortable lull in the conversation, Davey looked at me and grinned. "I lost my first tooth today, Daddy."

He opened his mouth, sticking his lower jaw out proudly to show me the gap.

"Ah... yes, which tooth is that?" I declared, resting his chin under my hand.

"The lower right incisor," Davey said, matter-of-factly.

"Davey and I have been brushing up on dental terms at bedtime. Haven't we, bud?"

Hannah's chuckle told me my quick wit wasn't enough to make up for my selfishness. "Alright, *Marathon Man*," she said, rolling her eyes.

"Mmm-hmm," he said.

"Well, you know what that means for tonight, don't you?" I asked.

"The tooth fairy isn't real, Dad," he said. "That's for babies!"

I nodded, perching my lower lip out. "Maybe, but statistically speaking, kids that believe get more money than deniers do. So, what are you, a believer... or a denier?"

"A believer," he said, the new gap in his grin showing again.

"That's better," I said. "A little imagination never hurts anyone, does it?"

As Hannah looked at me, my paranoia went into high gear and I all but convinced myself the Garashock 500 brand was emblazoned on my forehead, and she knew I'd succumbed. As we cruised through the rest of dinner, I found a way out, coming up with an excuse about needing to send an e-mail and made my quiet exit.

No man sets out to be absent as a father, but many of us are. Write that down and save it for later.

Grabbing a stubby beer bottle from the fridge, I slipped into our bedroom, wasting minutes away on my smartphone while I sipped, its cool burn taking me to a better place. I looked over at my nightstand and considered *Entertainment Weekly*, but instead took a double dose of my sleeping pills. Somewhere within five minutes, I drifted away, leaving the people I loved most in exchange for the overdue sleep I thought I deserved.

# MEDICINE MAN

I sat there in the lot, waiting for the client to arrive. East Region had become my district to manage, but I'd still venture back and forth between it and the West Region sales district. Exchanges in many of our deals weren't that meaningful. Medicine sold itself. People were sick, dying, and in need, and despite limited supply, there was money to be made both on and off the record. I'd go in the pill mills, leaving samples, charming the assistants regularly, and doing all I could to collect referral commissions. The market wasn't cutthroat, but it was dangerous. In the illegal drug trade, there are turf battles with nicks and scratches. In the white-collar drug trade, there are blood baths with decapitations and dismemberments.

Some of the offices I frequented were rundown in dire need of updates. From wood-paneled walls to rat droppings in corners, crackwhores, illegals, and vagrants lined up for services and treatments they couldn't receive elsewhere. I knew they'd size up my Rolex and Jimmy Choo's. I was convinced I'd eventually get jumped at one of my late afternoon stops as dusk neared. Somehow, it never happened.

Maybe I was paranoid. I'd begged the company to let me carry a weapon when I'd go into these dives, but the answer was always a curt no. I could have rebelled and never been caught, but their tracking methods were unconventional — making my knack for checking e-mail and other phone notifications an obligation.

I straightened my plaid necktie multiple times in the vanity mirror, touching up my hair with melted pomade I kept in the glovebox for windy days. As the client pulled up to our East Region meeting spot, I grabbed my briefcase, introduced myself, and escorted him into the building.

"So, you guys are renting in *here*?" he asked as we walked past a row of workers tagging and marking premium linens. "What's the connection?"

My eyes were drawn to the perfect symmetry of the factory. There's a finesse to bedsheets that many fail to appreciate, including me. Learning the difference between run-of-the-mill sheets in a big box store compared to a place like this is something you had to feel to understand.

I looked back at the client and smiled as we continued toward the rear. "Mori Olkov has exported fine Egyptian cotton sheets for years. This is one of his legacy franchises. We'll be sure to get you some complementary sets for your time."

"Ah. Well, that sounds nice."

As we walked past rows of plant workers and assembly line tools, we entered an unassuming, but vacant, office at the back of the building, its warm incandescent bulb buzzing loudly. There was a pan catching the drip of a leaking air handler that made our exchange less than professional keeping my own momentary neuroses on edge. We sat down at a plastic table with a matching set of metal chairs. I opened our catalog.

"So, why are we here?" the man asked.

"We still maintain our corporate HQ for day-to-day affairs, but considering its location, and the piss-poor parking options downtown, we came up with some... alternatives. I mean, as spread out as Middletown is, it just makes more sense if the east and west regions have their own rendezvous points to conduct business."

"I guess," the man replied, stroking his cheeks.

Olkov's strategies were unpredictable, but they kept me paid, so I asked few questions, knowing their answers would eventually lead to handcuffs. Operations had changed considerably the last few months.

"Direct sales are actually on the rise again in this area," I said, pointing to a map of clients before I turned the page. "We could offer you and your support partners a number of high-quality products for a fraction of the cost should you decide to purchase directly from us as your wholesaler."

"What processes do you follow to check the integrity of the product?" he asked.

"All medicines are FDA approved and laboratory tested, bar none. We just cut out the middleman. It's cleaner that way."

"And that's legal?" the man asked, squirming in the chair as it scraped the floor.

"As the wholesaler, we distribute using internal processes. Perfectly legal, just untraditional."

"How can you know for sure?" he asked.

"Years of proven salesmanship and happy customers," I said, licking my fingertips and thumbing through our catalog toward Garashock 500. "This one here, this is my best product. Our best seller."

The man nodded. "So I've heard. What's the markdown?"

"For you today, sir, I will give it to you at 20% below catalog price. That leaves a good profit margin."

"How does that keep you profitable?" he asked.

"You'll keep coming back, and when the client list grows, so does our supply chain demand because they talk about it. And with that comes discounted production costs. It's a knock-on effect. We take a gamble on you, hoping you are a repeat customer. You take a gamble on us as your wholesaler, hoping we continue to deliver you a top-notch product. Quite plainly, the 500s sell themselves and our clients love them."

The man nodded. "Well, I appreciate your candid demeanor," he said, looking over his shoulders. "No cameras in the room, right?"

"No, sir. No cameras."

He opened his briefcase with stacks of cash, end to end.

"Feel free to inspect," he said with a wide grin, a growing erraticism showing. I wondered if he was already in the Garashock 500 cult. "What will this get me?" he asked, licking his lips.

I eyeballed the cash, which looked to be about a hundred grand. "I'd say that's at least fifty cases of our finest."

The man stood up; his eyes were wide. "Great. When can you have it to me?"

"Give me a week. Where are we taking this?"

"Suit Warehouse Direct, on the lower east side. Take my card, and we'll square up on the details when you're ready."

"We'll call it the blue jacket special."

"The blue jacket special, huh?"

"Something like that," the man said, smiling. "We'll tuck it into the coat pocket and itemize it on the receipt as an alteration fee."

"I don't need specifics. The less I know, the better. It's a matter of conscience," I said, shaking his hand and having him fill out some information on a form. "Thanks for your business."

"Thank you."

We walked past a stocky plant worker near the entrance. I nodded my head toward her and held up two fingers. She tossed me two pre-packaged sets of the sheets.

"Oh, yes. This'll be nice," the man said.

"Your wife will love 'em. Trust me."

He shook his head and smiled. "My dog," he said, patting me on the shoulder twice. "Woof, woof."

I was ready to rip them away, knowing he'd stoop to such a low. I showed him to the door.

I made eye contact with the woman that handed me the sheets on the way back in. She tossed me another set.

"On me," she said. "Take them home and enjoy the difference."

Jean's voice chided within.

*It's the difference that sets you apart... or indifference. That separates the boys from the men, Benjamin. You sit there, trying to color inside all the lines, aiming to please, but you know the truth. Day can't be night.*

"Mr. Decker, sir. Are you okay?" she asked.

I looked back at the woman and nodded. "I think so. I'm a little short on sleep. It must be getting to me. Have a good afternoon."

"You, too, sir!"

# WEST SIDE

Our West Region rendezvous point was no improvement from the East Region's bedsheet factory. The Olkov's bought West Side Motel a few months ago and unofficially, under the table, a lot of our distribution work goes on down here. The enterprise was under a substantial audit and giving the façade we often did, those surveilling presumed West Side was doing the same thing it always had and continued to turn a blind eye. So that was our goal. To stay off the radar and operate without too much attention. West Side was a sleazy place that had long been an hourly hookup sort of joint. Mori gutted the first-floor rooms for Olkov, leaving the second floor for more of the other, the former stuff. Room number 142 was our usual meeting point.

A gorgeous blonde in a blue dress leaned over the side of the Mercedes in heels, showing more thigh than necessary, but this was all part of the act to minimize suspicion. Before I go any further, this is not what it looks like. This wasn't a breach of character or moral failure. I was there for work. Natasha ran Olkov Enterprises for the West Region, and because of the place's unassuming locale, we conducted a lot of business there. And by conducting business, I mean it. There's no double entendre, nothing cheeky here.

It was true. The Olkov's did business differently. Mori was unique, a real charmer. It wasn't the tough guy routine, rather the sophisticated businessman. No f-bombs or naked women lounging around. His likability went up 348% as a result.

He sat across from me in 142, the nicest room in West Side. The room was well-dressed, considering the tight quarters. Naturally, the king-size was graced with heavy threaded Egyptian cotton bedsheets, a modern 85" television lining the east wall, a commissioned painting of the Olkov family (many of whom remain in Russia), and an orange leather sofa that led Mori to many power naps after overindulgent lunches.

"Mori," I said, peeking out the window, "One day, they're going to notice. It may be time to move soon. A row of Mercedes parked outside this dump's a dead giveaway with the cops swarming next door at the Denny's every meal break."

Mori laughed as he lit up a Cuban cigar, pouring an indulgent helping of Cognac for the both of us. "Ben, Ben, you worry too much. Suspicious one, aren't you? Hmm-hmm."

The chuckle had begun to irritate me. It was never the "ha-ha" with the open mouth, but always the "hmm-hmm," mouth closed, smug faced. He did it too often. I figured it was the alcohol, but never the drugs. Mori never used, and I believe that's saying something about his commitment to the infamous, "Shoot straight. Make money."

I sighed, collecting a briefcase of cash, and another full of Garashock 500s. "I just don't want to... I don't want to see this thing go sideways. We're profiting big here, Mori. Too much of a good thing for too long is bound to collapse. It's not a matter of if, but when."

He puffed his cigar. "Large living in quiet space... aren't we, Ben?"

"Living large, and yes, it is a quiet space, but not so discrete."

"We have an agreement with the police. You know that, right?" he asked.

"It's not the police I'm concerned about. I'm talking about Feds. DEA. FDA. God knows who else. I feel them inching up my sleeve more every day."

"Don't you like the clash, though, the contrast? Dream American, yeah? Rags to riches. Dust to dust."

"Ashes to ashes. Dust to dust. That's what we'll be if we're not more careful."

"Hmm-hmm. You know what I mean. My English is pretty good, yeah?"

I nodded. “We sell a lot of pharmaceuticals. But what about the procurement?” I asked. “The audit trails… Eventually, somebody’s gonna catch on.”

“The investors in our business, Ben, they want to profit big. We give them wider cast to net.”

All the backwards expressions wore me out. I wasn’t normally so corrective, but perhaps the Cognac was getting to me, scrambling my inhibitions as the room wobbled around me and I drifted.

# HELL

I woke to screams.

Dear God.

It was Hannah. I was still adrift — the mix of Garashock, sleeping pills, and alcohol leaving me useless. Stumbling into the hall toward the kitchen, I worked to find composure, but it wasn't happening. My heart sank when I saw that Hannah had pulled the aspirin bottle from my bag and its lid was off on the counter, one of the little blue Garashock 500s missing.

I was a creature of habit. My aspirin was always in my bag and somehow, I was stupid enough in the moment earlier to forget Hannah would remember that. I plowed into Jake's room. Hannah and I locked eyes. I knew everything before I looked down. Our son was dead, and there was no amount of CPR, prayers, or wonder pills to bring him back. As Davey came in behind us, the reckless collision of tragedy and trauma forever became a fixture in my mind's eye.

I see the room over and over. Jake's body was nothing more than a shell, a glorified meat suit. That's what we called it with the boys to differentiate the body from the soul. People say the soul is invisible but look a dead body in the eye a few times and you'll see that's a misnomer.

The three of us embraced while the 911 call played out in slow motion on our speakerphone. Life as we knew it would forever be different.

I could have gone to the pharmacy. It was two blocks, a measly two blocks away, no more than eight hundred yards from my front door. I pictured myself going in there to get the aspirin, such a simple task. There was probably nothing more than an overworked, underpaid college student rifling through dirty magazines and counting dead flies on the windowsills, an open pack of Chiclets at the ready. As fate would have it, I had nothing but negligence to blame for Jake's death. The choice I made right then is one that I live with today. Only I would know why Jake was dead. That was only half the problem. The issue was deep-rooted and systemic. What I mean to say is that the cases, suits, and liabilities that tanked J&P, carried ambiguity in the public eye, but we knew what was happening.

Highly concentrated doses of Garashock were not only addictive but also fatal, a user's weight being a huge factor. A single pill for a two-hundred pounder like me was okay for a trip to la-la land, but the same for a ninety-eight-pound child was inevitably a deathtrap.

***

I failed to admit what killed Jake, and she blamed herself— acting as if her own negligence was to blame. Certainly, pondering on all the things we might have done to sort him out. Maybe another trip to the doctor, an admission to the hospital, an extra round of IV fluids in the arm, whatever might have made that little difference and kept him around. The acknowledgment that the warning signs of his death had been there all along and she just missed it.

*What kind of mother misses it?*

She would ramble about that for hours and I never knew what to say, leaving the ugly, unforgiving thought to plague her. I saw it in her eyes. I knew her. Keeping the truth beneath the surface would only drive us further apart. So, I don't know why I didn't just admit it. I wish I would have.

We would converse, and she would ruminate on the idea, and though it pained me to hold back, I never told her, or acknowledged I was under the influence myself that night either.

And somehow, I guess I did some blame-shifting to minimize it. It ate away at my insides, an unspecified sickness. If I was the hands, Hannah was the feet, and though we both were to blame in our own ways, it was my fault. My failure to admit such wore me down.

No project around the house could appease the hurt. The coroner didn't help either. Even the autopsy reflected Jake's cause-of-death as influenza. I had no peace. It was just another lazy evaluation of convenience. Convenient because he tested positive for the flu. The little blue pill killed the kid.

Hannah never remembered the pill looking different because she never turned the light on. It was 2 AM. Consider this, when you're sleepless and lonely, you miss details sometimes. And that part is my fault. I left her in the cold when she needed me most. Hannah was never negligent. No matter how many ways she beat herself up. I was. She was the desperate mother — half asleep, anxious to cure our son of a lingering discomfort. I was the bastard in the self-induced night-time coma. I needed to make changes quickly to escape the feelings of torment that hovered. It was a make-or-break sort of thing.

# DATE NIGHT

I parked the car outside the house as dusk encroached. All the lights in Jean's home were out, but the faint glow of a television shined from outside the edges of the curtains of the living room window.

Jean's voice hit me again.

*I'll just love seeing your perfect little family through my window.*

I went inside our house to greet Hannah and Davey.

"It's great to be home."

"I'm so glad," Hannah said, her face perfect and pristine. She donned a beautiful evening dress, and her hair was clipped back nicely. An unsubtle perfume reminded me she was expecting more from me than I'd planned. "How was your day?"

"Good enough. I made a few connections, sold some more 500s. What are you so dressed up for?"

"Ben, I texted you," she said, her glossy lips clamping together tightly.

"What?"

"Dad's coming over to watch Davey. He'll be here any minute so we can enjoy the evening out."

I sighed. I'd missed the message or forgotten, one of the two, and neither one was permissible.

"What's the matter? I coordinated all of it so you wouldn't have to," she said, her hand resting on her hip. Instead of flipping into confrontation mode, she remained cool, perhaps considerate of my long day.

"Nothing," I said, "just a little tired."

"Ben, I've got the whole night laid out. All you have to do is show up and I'll do the rest." Her voice and eyes told me different stories.

If I went with the voice, I was in good graces. If I went with the eyes, the couch would beckon for me later. Considering Bill Shatner's special to space would be on late that evening, I considered my decision a split second before I replied.

"Aye, captain. Thanks for setting that up."

"Dad will be here in five minutes. Get yourself in order, Ben Decker. A pretty lady wants to make you feel good tonight," she said, poking me in the stomach.

I smiled. "I'm glad to hear that." I wrapped my arms around her waist. "You look beautiful tonight."

Hannah grinned. "Tonight? And what am I every other night?"

"Beautiful."

"Smooth. I wouldn't use that as a pickup line, though."

Hal arrived, carrying in a Happy Meal for Davey. He and I had a quick exchange and I climbed into the car.

We pulled out of the driveway, and I looked at Hannah. "Does Jean have any kids? Husband?"

"I don't know. I went over there earlier to drop off the pie pan, but she wasn't home. Didn't notice evidence of anyone else. Just the dog."

"That little battery-powered Shi... Tzu? What's his name?"

Hannah laughed. "Gonzo."

"Pathetic excuse for a name. Come on."

We drove down the expressway, passing a couple of exits and the usual less-than-stellar scenery of Middletown.

"I've been wanting to talk to you about Davey."

"Oh?" I said, fumbling around with the radio dial.

"He's not being pushed hard enough right now. He's already at an eighth-grade reading level, Ben."

"Yeah. That's good. He's our *Real Genius* alright." I said. To say I was distracted would be an understatement. I sighed.

"What is it?"

"I'm still miffed Jean wouldn't say where she worked. Not all of us are stalkers, you know?"

"Ben, you're a salesman. You're one step away. Maybe she just wanted to get to know us a little. You know, make sure we aren't killers. You hear about that sometimes. Crazy couples, one feeding off the other, until something snaps and someone's dead."

"Maybe you're right. I'm not sure. I just... get a vibe."

Hannah scoffed. "You and your vibes. You know I don't like it when you talk about that. It weirds me out."

"Why? Because I'm usually right?"

"Yes, Ben. Because you're *always* right."

I smiled. The sarcasm was her way of playing as much as it was punishing. That mix kept me intrigued and engaged with her. Something about the simple moment reassured me Shatner's trip to space could wait.

"Fratelli's, right?" I asked. "Sorry, I guess I just assumed."

Hannah nodded. "You were going the right way. I knew you were still a step ahead."

"Do you mind?" I asked, turning the radio on to the local rap station. Eminem cursed every line like a smooth operator, but half the words were bleeped out, not giving the man his due rhyming credit.

"Since when do you like rap?"

"Since *8 Mile.* He's an everyman, not a villain."

"Oh."

Fratelli's came into view, and we entered the lot. I approached the valet. I studied Hannah's almond eyes. "Let them park it. I'm ready to eat," I said, throwing the keys to the driver.

Fratelli's was as close to Michelin Stars as Middletown could expect. Each tablecloth and linen were perfect and white, no steak sauce, wine stains, or loose salt or pepper left over from previous guests. No children or animals allowed. Immaculate to the point of a perfect health inspector rating its last six months. It was our go-to place on fancy date nights.

As we found our seat inside, Hannah studied the menu and I flicked through my phone, distracted.

"I thought you were starving. What's so important you have to pull that thing out again? You have me here, no kid, no distractions. Don't waste this. You know we need some time together."

"I'm sorry. Had a client trying to firm up some details on a deal. Let me get this sent out, then I'll put it on do-not-disturb."

"Fine."

The waiter approached.

"We'll share a bottle of the Moscato and the house bread tray. My husband's still... reviewing the menu," she said, a tone in her voice.

The waiter took notes and looked at me. I was admittedly more concerned with work than I was ordering a meal. "Very good. I'll be back to get your order in a moment with the wine and bread."

Hannah shook her head. "You have some nerve. Are you with me tonight?"

I remained lost in my own world swiping.

"Ben..."

"As Mel Bernstein says, 'every day above ground is a good day.'"

"Huh?"

"It should have been Frank Lopez. No one remembers Bernstein."

"Ben... I don't care and neither does anyone else."

"Alright, fine," I said, smiling. I put my phone down. "I'm sorry."

"Let's talk about real life for a change," she said. "Things have been tough lately."

"I'm the one that's out of line, not you. You're always trying to apologize and excuse my problems. Don't do that. We're all a work in progress."

The waiter approached the table, pouring the wine and presenting the bread.

"Thank you," I said, slicking my hair and rubbing the back of my neck.

"I'll take the rib eye, medium well, with a baked potato, and pinto beans."

"Very good," the waiter replied. He had a snootiness that annoyed me, but considering I was often there with Mori, too, I wouldn't push my luck. Saliva flavored food's overrated.

Hannah looked at the waiter and her tiny voice chirped, "I'll take the grilled chicken salad. Ranch dressing. Lots of it."

"We'll get this out as soon as we can. Anything else I can get you?"

I shook my head. "No, thank you."

Hannah sipped her Moscato. Her face soured.

"Not any good tonight, is it?" I asked.

"It's fine."

"Let's just order some tea."

Now that she had my attention, I'd lost hers.

"What's on your mind, honey?" I asked, finishing my wine.

"Jake," she said, starting to tear up. "I see him every day. Hear him. His little fingerprints everywhere," she said, the tear streaming down her cheek.

I reached across the table and rested my hand on top of hers. "It wasn't your fault."

"You can tell me that every day, Ben, but it doesn't change the fact he's gone. That void will never be filled again."

"You do a great job at hiding it, Hannah," I said.

"It's not fair. I don't want to keep up appearances. I'm still miserable, and you are, too. I mean, what are we supposed to do? Picking up the pieces isn't easy for anyone. I'm just thankful Davey's young enough not to fully grasp it. It's too much for a kid to carry."

The waiter brought our food over. The presentation was mediocre, the garnish misplaced, stale, and unworthy of its $38 price tag.

"Thanks," I said.

"Get you anything else?"

"Nope," I said, looking at Hannah and tapping her on the hand gently. "You need anything?"

"I'm fine."

"Fine is code language for don't badger, right?"

"I don't have to answer that. Do I?"

# TOOL MAN

5:47 PM.

Hannah approached the Mercedes while Davey sat on the porch swing. I wasn't expecting a car-side greeting.

"Hey, I need a favor."

"Sure," I said. "What's up?"

"It's actually for Jean."

I sighed and gritted my teeth. "Oh? What is it?"

"Issues with her washing machine."

"And you told her I was the man for the job? You know my track record on this kind of stuff. I'll be lucky if I don't burn the house down or lose a limb in the process."

"She's tight on money."

"Well, we can just pay someone for her. I don't want to do it."

"Just go over there, Ben. You can leave a better impression on her."

"Do you want that? Me by myself... in some other woman's house that I barely know? I always get nervous in these situations. You never know what someone's gonna say. They could tell an ugly lie that might ruin you."

"She's not going to do that, Ben. Get changed and go over there."

"Fine," I said, stepping out of the car.

"Thank you, Mr. Decker," she said.

I kissed her in case Jean was listening or watching and I was pretty sure she was. I patted Davey on the shoulder and went inside, changing into more labor-friendly attire.

I grabbed my toolbox, a prop I mostly kept for looks, walked past Hannah, and opened my eyes wide as I approached the front door — no words necessary. I went across the yard and knocked on Jean's door. She opened it immediately.

"Benjamin, it's so good to see you," she said in a throaty voice. She wasn't sauced, but clearly trying harder to leave an impression. "I was hoping you could come take a look. Follow me this way. It must be a belt going bad or something. I just thought a guy like you might have the tools to fix it."

"I'm no expert, but I'll do what I can," I said.

"I bet you will," she said.

She was wearing extra eye shadow, tighter fitting pants, and a low-cut blouse that day, all surely to grab more of my attention and tell me she could step up her game when she wanted to. This wasn't just speculation. The voice, the rhythm to her speech, the bounce in her step. I'd swear she played it ten years younger with me when Hannah wasn't around.

She was all smiles as she led me to the back of the house, which was remarkably tidier than the first time we stopped by. I guess something had her motivated. Gonzo yapped at me like always. Jean tossed him in the neighboring bedroom abruptly.

"Maybe you can just show me what's going on with it. That's probably the best way," I said, stepping back.

She turned the washing machine on, and it cycled through its first few steps without issue.

"Hmm... I don't see anything wrong with it right now," she said. "That's odd."

It was a front loader, so I was already on my knees to take a closer look as it cycled.

"Well, maybe it's this one," she said, moving uncomfortably close to me as she leaned over to adjust the knobs on the machine, a load of her unmentionables cycling through as she pressed against me for a second.

"Well, Jean, I'm not sure I see anything wrong. You said you think a belt's loose?"

"I'm sorry to waste your time, Benjamin."

She dropped her phone on the floor and bent over to grab it. She took her time getting up as if she were trying to draw more attention to herself. It was just another thing to bother me about her. She looked at me as I stood up and the look in her eyes told me she wanted me there by myself — I was a newfound crush.

I walked out of the laundry room and toward the front of the house.

"Ben, can I get you a drink? Fix you something to eat?" she asked.

I shook my head. "No thanks, Jean, I'm sure Hannah's got that covered."

"Hannah, or Chow Fung's?" she asked, cattily.

Hannah would have been offended, but I brushed it off. Jean's maneuvers troubled me, but minimizing and not enabling was the best approach, tactically speaking.

"If you see that... intermittent issue again with the machine, see if you can make a note of the time or record it on your phone or something, that'll give me more to work with."

I went out the door approaching our house. I turned around a second and spotted Jean watching me through the east window of 1739. She waved, pulling her curtains closed.

Going into the house, I found Hannah in the back bedroom painting. A mellow number from Lifehouse kept her company. She looked at me.

I raised my eyebrows.

"Well?" she asked.

I debated on what to share, what degree of detail. I figured I could manage.

"Well, I didn't see anything wrong with the machine. Jean was giddy as ever to have a man in her house, though. She was more dressed up than we'd ever seen her."

"Oh? And you noticed that, huh?"

"Hannah, she went from a two to a five. You're still my ten, baby."

"And you're still full of... stuff," she said, exaggerating our kid approved language.

"Yep!"

# UNRESOLVED

I laid restless in bed that night. Thinking of Jean and what she was after. It wasn't clear to me. I didn't think I was the object of her affection. It was an attention-seeking type of behavior like something in a psychology textbook. I waffled back and forth, hour after hour. And perhaps it was poetic that in what Mom once called the witching hour, I heard her voice, Jean's voice, loud and proud.

*Some people call you paranoid. I call you prepared. And anyone that crosses us ought to know we're ready and waiting to strike the second they do.*

*Maybe it's just the baggage of the past piled up and weighing us down, or maybe, it's you.*

*Yeah, maybe it's you.*

*Look at those ivory cheeks.*

*She thinks she's so damn perfect?*

*The posh Range Rover.*

*The designer handbag.*

*That perky ass.*

*The daily Starbucks fix.*

*The cute kid.*

*And she's all yours.*

*It must be nice.*

*I make myself sick watching. I don't know what's come over me. Sparks flying between us like I've never felt with a man, not even on my best days. Jean Jackson, love-struck by a traveling salesman. And I think of that... thing you have living with you. That disgusting excuse for a spouse. Benjamin, how much better you could do if you really wanted. You can do better. And here I am waiting, fifty-five steps from your front door.*

*You tie your curtains up, inviting me into your life, making the gross assumption I want to know how you live — to stare into your picture-perfect moments. I didn't ask for that.*

*Is it too much to ask of you to keep private things private?*

*I can't help but watch, green with envy, sick with some kind of parasite in the brain. It's unhealthy, but it's all I know to do, and cheaper than cable. Give me too much free time and a weird work schedule and this kind of thing happens. A tragedy, a ticket to home-wrecking — a rush I can never seem to satisfy. Step away from reality a minute and accept the fact that monotony creates monsters. Ha!*

I gasped, concluding I really knew nothing of Jean, or about anything. Hannah rolled over and put her arm around me.

"You okay?" she asked.

"Yeah. Just having trouble sleeping for some reason."

"You took your sleeping pills, right?"

"Yeah. Hopefully, they'll kick in soon. I love you, Hannah."

"I love you, too."

*And so do I!* Jean said, somewhere beneath the overnight hum of our air conditioner. Normally, for most of us, it's moments like this, you struggle. Where you can't define the origin of the voice, whether it's the one in your head or not.

# ROYAL FLUSH

My ears were still ringing when I woke the next morning. I had a few follow-ups with clients, then met Mori at Fratelli's. Though my role had changed in some ways, I still got my hands dirty, working to set the tone for the rest of my sales group that executives weren't above the law. The restaurant was quiet that afternoon.

Mori took advantage. From jokes to sleight of hand, the man was an enigma that forever pleased — maybe even a Russian Bill Clinton. I was waiting to spot Monica in a red dress that time.

I finished my salad while we waited for our filets.

"I don't think I have anything further to report," I said, sliding my client list over to Mori on a scratchpad documenting product and shipment amounts. The language was all in shorthand that only the two of us could dissect but gave enough context to get the point across. He pulled out his tablet and showed me a map flagged with pins dropped all over the West Region.

The waiter brought our meals, beautifully decorated on matching plates. The only difference, Mori's was bloody, and mine, well done.

"Natasha's got quite the handprint here, Ben," he said, thanking the waiter.

"Footprint, sir."

"Yes, uh, footprint," he said, swiping the tablet map across to the opposite side. Vodka was the natural choice for him at lunch hour. He was on his third shot while I struggled to finish my first. "A lot here in East Region, though. Lots of covers to ground."

I contemplated correcting him but decided against it. "Yes. We're working on it."

"Very good," he said, biting into his bloody filet.

"Okay. Well, I'll have the crew get out east the rest of the week and see what other kind of business we can drum up."

"Drum up?"

"Yes, expression. To collect."

"Yes. Drum up. I like that! I add to list," he said, smiling. "Ben Decker, you learned lesson today, right?"

"What lesson?"

"Never hassle Russian while he's eating. Hmm-hmm."

"Right. Mori, excuse me. I'll be right back," I said.

I found my way into the bathroom stall and flicked through my phone, securing another deal with a client on the west side, and prepping to wrap lunch. If I had a little more to talk about, I'd give Mori greater confidence in me. Reaching into my pocket, I felt my pill bottle.

Our teams grasped for straws to sell Garashock 500 legally, often bending and breaking rules to keep Olkov profitable. The fraudulence would come out eventually, but until then, we had to move as quickly as possible to avoid tailwinds.

I fumbled around in my pocket again, pulling the bottle out. It was some kind of fluke the pills ended up there, happenstance.

I needed something to take the edge off with Mori and vodka wasn't cutting it, something to close out the meeting with confidence. I unscrewed the lid. The pills beckoned in vulnerable moments. That's what scared me. Some unknown force hovering above or resting in the recesses of my brain was still poking and prodding to remind me what the pill could do for me. That uncontrolled addiction impulse took hold in an instant, and before I ended up back to square one within seconds, I poured the pills into the toilet and flushed it.

I was still drunk, but I was proud. I didn't give in. Considering the clock to my sober timer was reset after my last shot, I'd already disavowed any morality I promised before.

My mind wandered, knowing how many times I'd reassured my clients they wouldn't become addicted. One pill was all it took. The science proved it and that was what held it up from circulating to the masses beyond experimental phases. There it was, the itch, the tingle that summoned. Though the pills were somewhere in the depths of the plumbing of Fratelli's, they screamed for me. And Jean did, too.

*Why'd you do that? You know that edge... that itch... that feeling you have when things go wrong! Be a better steward, Benjamin!*

# WATER RESTRICTIONS

My commute home left me in some other dimension, I guess. Dimension is the wrong word, but I wasn't as present as I should be. As I came into the house, Hannah and I kissed and embraced. Before I could get to our bedroom to change, there was a tap at the front door.

"I'll get it," Hannah said, approaching and checking the peephole. "It's Jean."

"Hey, good neighbors," she said. "How are you doing?"

"We're fine. Is everything okay?"

"Well, that's what I'm here to talk to you about. I noticed you've been watering your lawn on Tuesdays and Thursdays and we're under phase three restrictions. Our days are Wednesdays and Fridays. I just didn't want you guys to get into it with the water man or get a citation."

"Oh, how considerate," Hannah said, looking back at me. "It's great to have a neighbor that cares enough to say something."

"Oh, it's nothing at all. I know you'd do the same for me."

Hannah nodded.

I came around the corner and approached the door. "I love my grass. I've got that on a timer. We'll get it adjusted. How's that washing machine?"

Jean looked away a second, sheepishly. "It's okay. I just need to screw around with you a little more."

"What?" I asked, looking away.

"I said, I just need to screw around with it a little more. I'm sorry... That probably isn't the most delicate way to put it. Daddy had a mouth on him. I guess some of that rubbed off on me, too. I better get on."

"You better," Hannah said.

"I've got my tools. Try the recording trick. If you can get it on camera, that might give us more to... 'screw around' with."

Jean nodded with a big grin. "Yeah, I'll try that."

"Would you like to stay over for dinner?" I asked. "We're gonna order some... Chow Fung's."

"Oh, I wouldn't want to impose."

Hannah shook her head. "Oh, Jean, you wouldn't be.

Jean looked down at her watch. "Well, I better get on. Y'all have a good night. Thanks for the dinner invite. Maybe another time."

As she walked out of the house and closed the door, my eyes met with Hannah's.

"What the hell is going on? Why is Jean acting like a giddy schoolgirl around you? Why is she 'screwing around' with you?"

"I don't know. I swear. I really don't. She's just crazy. She did that on purpose, you know?"

"Why do you say that?"

"She pulled a similar maneuver the other day when I went over there to check her washing machine."

"Check her washing machine? Is that code language? Why didn't you say anything?"

"You know she's not my type."

Hannah's posture eased up. "Okay. You're sure there's nothing else you want to tell me? Anything you left out after your 'checkup' with her?"

"Nothing else. You?"

"Nope," she said.

***

The routine felt predictable. My mind only roamed as I worked to doze off. We had an episode of *Cheers* on in the background, but I'm not sure either of us were watching. Maybe we just hissed when the laugh track cued us.

Jean's voice. It was waiting to strike again somewhere inside. I wasn't ready. I had no shields. No protective coverings. She'd invaded. Everyone couldn't be crazier than I was. It wasn't fair to think that way. It made more sense for it to just be me, my conscience in some sort of momentary psychosis. Sleep deprivation.

That's what it was. A side-effect of sleep deprivation. A chemical reaction to the sleeping pills. No. I'd rather unravel things logically, and if it ends up a conspiracy then shit, we're all screwed — every last one of us 'til the aliens probe us, and we end up the goo in some pizza pocket on another planet.

Admitting it would take a delicate touch. And as of late, I seemed to have everything but that.

Jean's affirmation ran through my head again.

*You're not paranoid. Just prepared.*

When you found yourself trapped in a situation like I was, the only way out was through bringing what was in the dark into the open. So, as I prepared what I might say to Hannah, I could only fathom a long American highway crumbling away in a spiral bound for hell. I'd work to sidestep it. The question was how.

# DEAD MEMORIES

I pulled into 1737. There was no one to greet me — no pot of coffee brewing or meal, cooked or ordered. Davey was already tucked in for the night, probably hours ago. Hannah sat in her studio with the lights dim, a white canvas that appeared nothing but black, the radio playing a mellow Coldplay number. I waved. She looked at me, her lips giving half a grin that dropped back into a frown. I approached her, resting my arm on her shoulder. It didn't take words. Shared presence was enough, reassuring us despite recent adversities, we longed for connection.

"I'm sorry. I had deals that kept me out later than I planned."

Hannah's eyes were hollow, wallowing in an overwhelming reality I struggled to acknowledge or relate to entirely. It wasn't the loss of Jake, but male and female differences.

I sat next to her and sighed. I didn't know where to direct the conversation. After a continued silent treatment, I turned to a Top 100 movie periodical instead, waiting for her to make the next move. I couldn't read a word. The magazine was just a prop. Truth was, we rarely spoke of the past, but it defined the bulk of our problems. Our wedding had been quiet — without our parents' blessing — a complicated sort of mess.

As I looked over at Hannah again, my mind wandered to Jake's funeral. It was the only time we'd seen Patricia in years, and then at hers, a month later. The anxiety of death was enough. Making the call to notify her was no easier. I guess if we want to get technical, something changed after Patricia died. Hal opened up—admitting he longed for a relationship with us and telling us Patricia was the one holding him back and that he hoped he could bridge the gap for the years lost, but it was just never enough. They never knew Jake. And that was something that still left unresolved hurt, especially between him and Hannah.

On the surface, Hal and Patricia were decent people who earned a respectable wage, the best kind of Protestants. Even to the point that they avoided a stocked liquor cabinet when times got tough. Hannah's mother got to her because of a particularity in keeping things tidy. That wasn't what drove them apart. Instead, it was a single incident where her mother lost her cool and told Hannah to "rot in hell." The matter seemed inconsequential. In fact, I believe it was more a political preference on a social issue than anything else, but nonetheless, an item so divisive they dissociated with one another entirely. It was just the kind of argument that tears families apart. I say po-tay-to. You say po-tah-to. That kind of nonsense.

The words we exchanged after Jake's funeral service were short and simple, but never enough to resuscitate our relationship with them, not by a longshot. Patricia was weary. Hal, slimmer and more spastic than I recalled, maybe some kind of undiagnosed hyperthyroidism or hypertension. Being their only child, I think Hannah wondered why they made so little effort to connect.

As for the wake, the last place we'd seen the shell of Jake, the pews of the Methodist church were in perfect symmetry. The carpets a kind of scarlet that matched Christ's blood or an ideal way to hide stains from weekly communion. The years of fade and foot traffic from ushers and deacons had worn away its brightest sheen, leaving it a dull burgundy.

Hannah and I opted for an open casket but couldn't bear to look. She and I wondered about the man Jake would've become.

Of his height and his stature.

Where he might attend college or his major.

The trade he would have pursued.

These thoughts would never leave us entirely, always resting somewhere in the recesses of our darkest moments.

His voice having never changed or cracked.

His body a mere four foot ten.

His weight still beneath the century mark.

His freckled cheeks, youthful but lifeless.

A mortician can only do so much. And as the soul moves on, the empty body's always unrecognizable.

I think Hannah was thrown by my demeanor that day. I didn't show emotion well and remained largely private in the grieving process, something she was still holding against me. She never admitted it, but somewhere within, it remained a trigger. I'd always been reluctant to over-emote in public, and though Hannah may have grown used to this with time, it left her unsure of how I felt because I didn't talk about it with her as much as I should have.

The reverend stood somber — the audience still in denial of the stark reality that loomed. Nothing would bring Jake back. I think Hannah felt she missed her chance to love him at her best. I know I did. I pressed my hands in front of my eyes, the dull voice of the minister fading away to the previous Thursday when we found him, every parent's most horrifying terror. There was no reconciling it.

The brochure at therapy told us a fast-track to divorce court was excusable. A child's death — a life changer, a deal-breaker, a path to a life of endless depression and worry.

Of guilt.

Of sorrow.

And just plain paranoia.

The worst kind of it, too.

That feeling in the pit of the stomach that Davey could drop dead just the same and it would be just the two of us withering away and bickering, all our secrets still intact. On the monkey bars, behind the school, on the bus, or even by a rattlesnake coiled up in the backyard under the playset.

I came back to the moment, realizing I'd lost a few minutes as Hannah chipped away at the black paint with a pointed tip, exposing a multicolored hue beneath.

"That looks beautiful," I said. "Wow."

"I guess," she said, her face flat and emotionless.

"I wanted to ask you how you were feeling about things. It's just felt a little... stale around here lately."

Her eyes told me she was processing. I could only imagine. I chose the wrong word at the worst possible time. I'm sure her thoughts were racing.

*What did stale mean? What was I getting at? Was she giving me what I needed? Was she taking care of Davey? Was the house clean enough? What else did I want?*

"I'm alright," she said. "Define stale."

"It just seems like you're falling back into one of your moods."

"My moods? What do you mean by that?" she asked, dropping her eyebrows.

"I don't know. You just seem... disconnected."

"Look who's talking. You're always busy with work. You rarely connect with Davey, always on meetings with clients, or on your damn phone! Don't lecture me on disconnect."

I shook my head. "I came in to check on you. Not put you on a witness stand."

"Well, you're not doing a very good job at that... I'll get over it. It comes in waves with Jake. You know that."

"I love you," I said, in hopes of changing gears.

"I love you, too," she replied, the tone in her voice all wrong.

My comment was haphazard — another royal screw up. And in that moment, there seemed enough resolve to excuse myself from the room and quietly make my way toward the television and the couch.

# FRIEND FOR DINNER

My phone was ringing. It was Hannah.

"Hello?"

"I invited Jean for dinner," she said.

"Oh? Why?"

"I just feel like we've gotten off on the wrong foot. Maybe a second chance is all she needs."

"She accepted?"

"Yeah," she said. "She sounded excited."

"Great," I lied. "I'll be home in a few."

Getting Jean on our side was a necessary evil. It was better that I acclimate.

My ride home was a blur. Buildings remained out of focus. Street signs were off kilter. Pedestrians were nothing more than a nuisance. And I knew that evening's encounter would change everything.

***

I pulled in. I was an hour late. Jean's Roadmaster was parked next door as dusty and dirty as ever. She sat at the kitchen table across from Davey and Hannah in the seat next to mine. I took a deep breath and grabbed my work bag. I needed words. I needed ways to ground myself. It wouldn't be easy.

"Hey, guys," I said, coming in the door.

"Hey!" they said in unison.

"I'm sorry for running late," I said, kissing Hannah on the cheek and sitting down.

"Cluck cluck," Hannah said, pushing an order of fried chicken toward me.

I patted Davey on the shoulder and smiled at Jean.

She grinned.

"Well? How's it going, then?" I asked.

"Going fine." Hannah said. "Jean was just telling us about the neighbors."

"Oh?"

"Yeah," Jean said, placing her chicken on her plate. "You got to watch out with these folks around here. The people behind y'all are thugs. The guy next to me's a creep. And that little biddy catty-corner and down the lane's just a busybody yapping on the phone all day to her mother about how bad my yard looks."

"Is that right?" I asked, looking at Hannah. "You ever tried fertilizer?"

"Ricky did. It just didn't work."

"Well, maybe you just have winter grass. You need something heartier. You know, the heat around here..."

"Look at the expert," she said. "Hannah, you've got a keeper."

Hannah chuckled. "Yeah, maybe so. Ben loves him some green grass."

Davey looked at Jean. "Well, you know, my teacher says people that mind their own business stay out of trouble."

Jean smiled. "Yeah. Well, that's true. I wish a few more people around here understood that."

"What do you mean?" Hannah asked. "Have you had trouble with people harassing you?"

"Oh, I don't know. Just a feeling I get sometimes."

"Well, always assume the best. People get misunderstood all the time," Hannah said.

Jean finished her chicken. "Maybe so. Hannah, you're a breath of fresh air."

Hannah blushed. "Thank you. Well, we're right next door if you ever need anything."

"I know it. Thank *you*!" Jean said.

I smiled at Hannah. The comment didn't match what I would have expected from her.

"That's my better half!" I said.

# COFFEE TALK

Work the next day was forgettable.

Broken water machine.

Bob Dowdy remaining obnoxious with my DVD copy of *Mystery Men.*

Mori smoking cigars.

Rent-a-cop walking the hallways, hopelessly wandering, trying to bust one of us.

And me dodging and ducking all the above in hopes of finding peace of mind. I tried music, a guided meditation, and even laid off coffee, but nothing helped.

Jake sat in my office last fall, looking at my corporate accolades of which there were plenty. I had a wall of employee of the month awards, the one-year plaque, the five-year plaque, the ten-year plaque, and the J&P branding iron.

"Dad, are you ever going to do something different?"

I glanced down at my reports. "I don't know, bud."

"You just seem like you're not that excited about your job, anymore."

"Well, you know, sometimes a change of scenery can really improve things," I said. "Maybe I can ask for one of those corner offices once I get that big promotion, a window would be nice."

"Would that be enough?"

I sighed and patted him on the shoulder. "I don't know. Why do you have to be so perceptive?"

"Mom."

"She keeps all of us sharp, doesn't she?"

Jake picked up my "Employee of the Year" company clock from five years ago that sat on the corner of my desk.

"You're pretty good at what you do, aren't you?"

I closed my eyes.

***

A few client calls later, it was quitting time. I guess I'd zoned out.

The ride home was quiet. Too quiet. Turning on the car stereo made it worse, though.

I pulled into the driveway. Hannah had the curtains drawn and I could see through the kitchen window. We had a guest. And there was some part of me that hoped Jean could be friends with Hannah. It would be convenient. I wasn't ready to let my guard down, though. I couldn't.

She and Jean were sitting at the kitchen table with mugs of coffee, their faces pinker than usual from what I can only assume was extended periods of laughing which is what they were doing when I came inside. Hannah and I locked eyes as I came through the front door. I kissed her and waved toward Jean. She must have caught a whiff of the Cognac from lunch because she glared at me. Jean might have, too.

"Looks like y'all are having a pleasant chat?"

"We are," Hannah said. "How was work today?"

"Good enough," I replied, smiling at Jean and then back at Hannah as she sipped her coffee.

"And how are you, Miss Jean?"

"Good enough," she said, mimicking me. She and Hannah burst into laughter.

"Well, I'll let you gals finish your coffee. I've got a yard to cut," I said.

Hannah nodded. "Davey's on his playset back there. Send him inside once you get close to him."

The reactions seemed unnatural, and normally I wouldn't care. But things with Jean just kept weaving and wobbling us all sorts of directions I couldn't have expected. She'd been so cold and unwelcoming the first time we met, turned hospitable, then flirty, and now acting like she's old friends with my wife. I couldn't seem to shake the feeling that something wasn't right.

My thoughts were jumbled but as much as I wanted to follow the adage, "innocent until proven guilty," we didn't know Jean, nor what she was capable of. The idea that she could have such an influence on the delicate woman I loved when I wasn't around concerned me. How could I look out for Hannah without sounding overprotective?

***

I gave up on admitting it. I had to figure out what the deal was. My restlessness was out of control. Physical exertion wasn't enough. Dropping alcohol shortened my fuse. Reducing sugar left hankerings at obscure hours. And I still felt lost. We got into bed that night. I glanced at Matthew McConaughey's autobiography on my Kindle while Hannah flipped through a home décor magazine. Our lamplights matched, but the bulbs didn't. Mine was fluorescent white while hers was warmer colored. I'm sure she knew I wasn't reading, but I wasn't ready to break the silence. I was ready for her to talk first for once.

"Well, how are things going, Ben?" she asked.

"Okay," I replied, appearing focused on my eBook as I swiped the screen.

"Are you sure? You were acting kind of strange after work."

"Just a stressful day in the field. Nothing worth mentioning. You and Jean had a pleasant visit?"

"Yeah. It was good."

I waited for her to articulate, so I didn't seem like an interrogator. The answers and clarity hovered in the sky somewhere in a place she wasn't ready to share.

"Good to hear," I said. "Any secrets we should know about?"

"Oh, who knows, Ben? She was friendly enough. Told me a little about her mother, the changes happening around town, and the miraculous turnaround they made on this place before we moved in."

"Miraculous?"

"Yeah. Just that the previous residents had trashed it. More of what she told us the other day."

"All this coming from a woman whose home... for lack of a better word is trashed? I don't see how she doesn't see the irony."

"Look at you, judge. You don't know her well enough to poke fun like that."

I scoffed softly. "And you do? What does she do? Who are her friends? Does she have kids?"

"Ben, I'm sure those things will come out in due time. It's not really my place to probe her."

"Well, be on your guard. Pay attention to what she says and asks. And don't volunteer more about us than what's appropriate."

"Thanks for the lecture, Dad!" she said, dropping her magazine on the floor. "Is there so much to hide?"

"No. It's not that. It's quid pro quo. I don't like oversharing until I have a handle on someone. We don't have that with her yet."

"We've been over this, already," she said. "Unless you've got something significant to share that you know about, I don't see why she's any threat to you. Can't I have a friend? Is that okay with you?"

I scoffed. "That's not what this is about. She's a divorcee. Sometimes, they're opportunists," I said.

"How dare you say that? He could have been an abuser, a cheater, or an alcoholic. Any number of good reasons."

"Or bad ones..." I said. "Is that your shortlist? Couldn't she have been one of those things, too?"

"That should be everyone's shortlist, asshat."

I shook my head. "There's another kind of person, Hannah. They play the victim card all night long. And then they burn you up once they've sucked you dry and exploited you. I want to keep each other honest. We've been hanging around each other long enough to do that, haven't we? Don't sell me short. I want you to be happy. I just want to be careful. Anyone that's a new friend overnight should have a trial period."

I rolled over and turned off my lamp. Grabbing my sleeping pills on the nightstand I crunched them up, hoping for a faster release. There was no simple way to doze off, but I faked it a while until she finally did. Our honeymoon phase in the new house ended as quickly as it arrived.

***

It was always the damn witching hour, 3AM. The air conditioner turned off, and the alarm clock flickered as I heard Miss Jean.

*Benjamin Decker. Crunch. Crunch. Crunch. Too bad those pills weren't blue... don't you sweat it... just 'cause I know your secret doesn't mean we can't still be friends? You better play nice when I come to visit. Or I might just have to tell someone.*

# NOCTURNAL WANDERING

When life hits you with the unexpected, you have two options: cower in the corner or run like hell. Though there's comfort in choosing one or the other for a short period, the payoff eventually fails.

I'm not saying there were moments you didn't enjoy it, but there were certainly occurrences that kept you guessing. You'd go to Denny's, wander the aisles of Rocko's Pawn and Loan, and on nights when you were really out of sorts, you'd test out different soda and candy mashups at the Gas 'n Sip pushing 500s samples to clerks and traveling patrons. Some nights, you'd even stand at the back near the lottery station doing crossword puzzles and call out the ones that stumped you.

"Rhymes with Kalamazoo."

They'd answer, "*Mr. Magoo*," but any form of facepalming was frowned upon.

The characters that came out of the woodwork in these hours and places — they were enough to leave anyone scratching their head, maybe even watching their back.

Had you been shanked? No. Were you frisked? Yes.

You came up with an escape plan. It wasn't as hard as you thought. There was some middle of the night sort of grace that happens that you get at no other time of day and with the help of convenience store snacks and a Route 44. You ended up the guy ahead, mapping your own destiny and path to victory.

You'd converse like you knew them. You'd walk down a dark alley and then all of the sudden a jerk in a gray hoodie's lunging at you with a knife to your throat.

"I'm gonna gut you up real good, pretty boy."

You kept your cool. "I know you would, but you know something? I just found the perfect sugar rush at the Gas 'n Sip. Can I show you what it is?"

They studied you a second, maybe even cocked their head sideways, giving you the once-over. That was half the battle. The other was getting them to move past you and on to the soda fountain. If you played your cards right, you might even end up exchanging numbers. Whether you called each other back or not, it didn't matter. You'd run into each other again. It was your own little sleepless anonymous group.

Whatever you had to do to quiet those racing thoughts. Sometimes, it all felt hazy and blue. You were walking to your car, spotted a flyer on your windshield, and bartered with the guys offering to pave your driveway, not for goods or services, but to let them practice fortune telling in the back seat of a Prius by a guy that went by Ned from 9 to 5 and Ted from 5 to 9. And that's when your feelings of inadequacy reduced. You felt normal. You didn't think about your fortune, good or bad. It was just fortune. And it was the wheeling and dealing that came after that was the ride. You thrived, but as the nights escaped you, so did the peace.

# CHANGING SEASONS

I raked the leaves in the backyard. There were thousands. I bagged them methodically at first and then grew lazy of the strategy when it filled our garbage bin, and I hadn't completed a fourth of it. I moved toward the garage and pulled out the blower. If I could blow enough of the leaves behind it, I could show my St. Augustine off again. Round after round, battery change after battery change. I didn't want to mess with gas or oil, but I'd do batteries all day long.

Davey hung upside down on his playset across the yard, calling out for my attention every fifteen seconds. I'd nod my head, act like I saw him, and keep working. I felt a gut punch, remembering Jake as he helped me at the other house last fall. I imagined him next to me helping in our new yard. It was just all the things a grieving parent hoped for in moments like this — some over-idealized father/son bond, a meaningful bit of advice, and your kid looking up and validating that you poured into them in a memorable and intentional way. I snapped out of it and went over to Davey, blowing the leaves and his hair around. He just smiled at me and giggled.

"I love you, bud," I said.

"I love you, Daddy."

As we made eye contact, there was a moment I convinced myself we'd bonded. Then I went back to the garage to hang up the blower and recharge the battery.

I came inside to laughter. Jean was over again and the two seemed even more casual this time than the last.

"Hey, ladies. What's new?" I asked, smiling at them, and moving toward Hannah for a kiss.

Jean sipped her coffee and grinned. "Oh, Benjamin, just a walk down memory lane."

"I only wish we'd met sooner," I said, grinning at Hannah.

Hannah laughed. "Sixteen years is pretty good. We were just discussing how you and I met."

"You were? It seemed funnier than that."

"Yeah."

"And remind me, what's your flavor of that story?" I asked.

"At the church social. You were the charmer," Jean said, chuckling.

"Oh, right, right."

"You were eyeing the vegetable tray, tried some pathetic pickup line from *Cocktail*. And yet, somehow, you left a lasting impression, a strange blend of shyness and coyness. You lit up the room with your charm, that sense of humor never overwhelming and the underlying melancholy, that was your ultimate relatability."

"Wow," I said, laughing. "That's almost... poetic. If that's the language Hannah used, I don't want to do myself any injustices. Tell us more about you, Miss Jean."

"I've lived next door forty-eight years. Fell on hard times and we just parceled it out piece by piece."

"Okay," I replied, taking Hannah by the hand. "And then?"

"And then I met Ricky..."

"Yeah?"

She sipped her coffee. "Yeah, we had some good times, some not so good ones, and then called it quits."

"Well," I replied, struggling to be empathetic, "I guess you're both in a better place on your own, then?"

"We had things bogging us down. And to make matters worse, he hooked up with a red-headed bimbo from Sacramento."

"Yeah, I'm more of a brunette from Oakland man myself..."

Jean sat stone-faced.

"Just kidding."

Hannah squeezed my hand. "I'm sorry. We didn't mean to butt into your business."

"That's okay," she said. "You really are a kidder, Benjamin. I like that. I better get going. Got to get on to work."

"Where's that again?" I asked.

"I could tell ya, but I'd have to kill ya," she said, the look in her eyes cinching it for me.

"Oh? Top secret stuff, huh?"

"Something like that," she said, smiling.

She walked across the yard and jumped into the Roadmaster, speeding away faster than I would have expected as it backfired.

I looked over at Hannah and poured myself a cup of coffee. "The church social?"

"Yeah. Those were happy memories, Ben."

"Yeah. I guess they were."

"Want to take Davey to dinner tonight?"

"Maybe *after* your shower. You have a leaf in your hair."

***

My thoughts raced on about Jean throughout the overnight hours. She was "Miss Jean" in my subconscious, but there weren't enough years between us to give her that differentiation.

Maybe I was reading into it too much, but Jean was elusive. I didn't know how a woman I'd shared such few words with could take such a hold. It wasn't obsession, nor envy. It was something archaic, buried deep — manipulating my time, space, and matter in ways I couldn't understand, and probably shouldn't. It was never jarring, but subtle, like termites hollowing out a home's middle just before it caved in, and you slept. I heard her voice again, just beneath the sound of the air conditioner.

*I don't know where to go. I don't know what to do. The only place to run, Benjamin, is with you.*

She sang.

*CONSIDER THIS // MY CONFESSION.*
*MY LIES BIRTHED IN YOU.*
*MY CONSCIENCE OVERRUN // WITH GUILT YOU'LL NEVER KNOW.*

*THE BLOOD DRIPPING FROM YOUR HEART // AND SPILLING INTO MINE!*

Her voice burrowed deeper and deeper like the ear mite I never wanted to know.

You only deny the existence of this sort of thing until you can't. Until you see it for yourself. That's the whole point, isn't it? To ye of little faith, there's no reward, only damnation. If commentary becomes religious, maybe it's because it's supposed to. Or perhaps it's always there, and you didn't look — your cultural attenuators only self-seeking. It isn't a senseless rant. This is your reality.

# MY OWN INVESTIGATION

Hannah and I finished our breakfast quinoa after Davey left for school. Her eyes were sunken beyond sleep deprivation. I didn't know how to broach the subject without being offensive.

"You alright?" I asked.

"I don't know."

"What's going on?"

"I just... haven't found my element with my painting. I need that muse. You know?"

I carried our bowls to the sink and dropped them in. "Yeah. I hear that. Sometimes the answer's right in front of you. You just need something to light the fire... that little spark."

"Yeah," she said, looking out the dining room window toward Jean's house. "I think I've got something."

"Yeah?"

She nodded. "I'll fire up Matchbox Twenty and see where it takes me."

I smiled. "Don't let me get in your way. I'll look forward to seeing what you come up with. I love you," I said, leaning in to kiss her, and approaching the front door.

"I love you, Ben."

Sitting in my car, I reviewed my sales reports, prepping to go inside. I turned down the talk radio during the commercial break while Jean's voice came front and center.

*I dare you to come and find me. It's not cat and mouse. It's mouse and mouse. You know what I mean. Don't ya?*

I concluded my next transaction and went on toward the office. After I logged my reports in the system and dodged Bob Dowdy in the breakroom, I started digging. Something I remembered from a job I had before reminded me that divorce records were public. It wouldn't take much to find Jean's ex, and that might help. A few internet searches led me to Ricky, the man she spoke of briefly.

Hannah's speculation was right. The divorce was still fresh, an open wound. As much as it might seem borderline psychotic for me to dig so quickly, I needed to calm my neuroses — to rationalize my fixation with Jean. Either that or check myself into a room with padded walls. I needed validation. If Ricky would solidify that, I'd finally get somewhere. If he didn't, I could book my ticket on the crazy train with Ozzy, and we'd all be on our merry way.

I got online, rolling my way through the county appraisal district page, and sure enough, one Ricky Jackson was a resident at Lot 37 in the Hill Haven Trailer Park — his little slice of heaven. A few Facebook searches took me to his employer, a maintenance company called Second Chances that reportedly fixed everything from hotel furniture to over-worn box springs. End of the day, I was just looking for an in. I didn't want anyone concerned I was a stalker. It was easier to pose as a recruiter. They're a little that way, right?

*I found your resume online and just wanted to see if you'd be interested in a role I had open for someone with your skill set.*

Or a realtor. That felt natural.

*Did you know that your mobile home has a rare serial number and is a limited edition? I have a prospective buyer ready and willing to pay double for that doublewide. Let's grab a coffee.*

At some point, I realized the difference between me and Jean might not be so different. Maybe the whole reason I thought she was crazy was because I was, and I sensed we were kindred spirits. That there were no coincidences. That we were linked. Do enough mind acrobatics on this sort of situation, and you realize you easily become the doomed tool of your own worst thoughts.

I contemplated telling him the truth and asking questions. What would that offer? Would he just call Jean and alert her? Or would he be ready to sing like a pinned-up canary and tell me what we'd gotten ourselves into? Either way, there was potential. Whether fun or trouble, I was unsure.

At that moment, I was a thrill seeker. And it's for that reason, I concluded, I was a realtor. This was the moment I changed up my narrative. Why does he have to own a rare trailer with a special serial number? That's farfetched. I could just call him and tell him I'm looking at buying 1737, and that he was listed as an associate to the previous owner, which is mostly true. An ex-mother-in-law counted. Yeah. That was less psycho. My subscription to Neighborbuddy got me a phone number.

I was anxious about traceability, so I bought a burner phone. No trace, no tell. I dialed, and he never answered. I wasn't surprised. I should have been more prepared to leave a message. Improvising on a machine takes a delicate touch. Thank God I'm a salesman.

"Hey there, this is for Mr. Ricky Jackson. My name's Will Haggard. I'm a realtor local to the Middletown area and had you listed a close associate to the address 1739 17th Street and the house next to it, 1737. I was wondering if you might have time to answer a few questions. I have a client interested in buying that property after the renovations and they want to follow up on a few things before making an offer. Call me back at this number when you have a chance."

I hung up. I didn't know when to expect a call, or rather, if to expect one. In all reality, he had no good reason to call back. Unless he just had nothing better to do. Or was just a really nice guy. Then again, I did have a voice that sticks, like someone who could hack it on the radio if he wanted to. For some, that's more an attraction than a repellent.

***

I came home an hour after leaving the message and still had no call.

Hannah and I shared Chow Fung's for dinner, and I brought Davey a Happy Meal. It was family movie night. *Beetlejuice* seemed appropriate considering the time of year.

I looked over at Hannah. She was more focused on the screen than anything else. "Fun fact: Beetlejuice only has seventeen minutes of screen time the entire film."

"Yeah. I guess that's true," she said, disengaged.

"It must be nice to be the star of a movie and only work eighteen percent of the time."

"Can you just shut up and watch?"

"Fine."

As I took another bite, I felt the burner vibrating in my pocket. I didn't think explaining why I had it to Hannah would be justifiable, so it made more sense to excuse myself abruptly in hopes she didn't differentiate it from my normal phone.

"I'm sorry, I've got to take a call."

"Who is it?" she asked.

"No one of consequence. I'll be right back."

It was a stupid reply. I could have said any other name and it would have brought less attention to it. I went into our room and shut the door.

The caller ID on the screen told me I had Ricky.

"Hello."

"Hey, this is Ricky Jackson. I'm returning your call."

"Yes, sir. Thanks. I was just wanting to ask you a few questions about a property. I showed you as a next of kin or close associate."

"Not anymore I'm not."

"Oh. Well, do you know who I might get in touch with, then? I've tried ringing the lady next door and she won't answer."

"That doesn't surprise me one bit," he said. "Typical."

"I'm sorry?"

"That's my ex, Jean. She's not a great... people person."

"Well, maybe you can put in a word for me? You know, just to let her know I don't bite."

"We're not on good terms. My current wife won't let me have any more to do with her. She's dead to me."

"Oh. Well, I'm sorry to hear that."

"Life goes on," he said. "What can you do?"

"Well, I'll cut to the chase. Do you mind talking to me about 1737 17th Street? What do you know about it?"

"Alright... Jean's mother lived in there a while. When she died, the inheritance money ran out, and Jean had to sell it. It got us out of debt, though. At least until... 'til... I'm sorry."

"I'm sorry, you don't have to continue if it's a sore subject."

"Until our son died about a year ago."

"Oh, God. I'm sorry."

"Yeah. It's not an easy thing to talk about."

"I understand," I said. "I really do. We lost our son, too. He was ten."

My personal life had slipped into my fantasy life.

"Your local, right?" he asked.

"Yeah."

"Want to have a drink sometime? I can't really talk to my wife about this, and I'm too much of a cheap ass to pay for therapy."

"Yeah. I'd like that," I replied.

"Let's grab a pint at the IronWorks. You free next Thursday?"

"I'll make some time."

Before I could continue, Hannah plowed into the door. "Who are you talking to?"

"I've got to go, bye."

I slid the phone in my pocket.

"Hannah, it's a... a client."

"What's that phone? I haven't seen that before. Are you hiding something from me?"

I shook my head. "Of course not."

"It's a burner phone, Hannah. The client is a close associate of Mori's, and there were concerns of retaliation if the deal went sideways."

"Retaliation? Ben, you're scaring me. Mori approves of burner phones?"

"In this case he does."

"Can I see it, please? If there's nothing to hide, then you've got nothing to worry about, right?"

"He's the only guy I've called. Call him back if you want. I don't care. Just one small favor," I said, handing it over.

She staged the screen for the callback.

"What's that?"

"Don't start the next Cold War with this guy. He drives a hard bargain."

She turned the screen off and tossed the burner phone back to me.

"I already knew who you were calling, anyway."

"Yeah?"

She leaned in close to my ear and whispered, "Beetlejuice... Beetlejuice... Beet..."

# NEW SUBSCRIPTION

I arrived home. The Mercedes was freshly washed, I had the top down, and the Pixies blared off key but on tempo. Hannah was on the couch inside, visiting with Jean again. Our single-paned windows weren't enough to squash the volume of their laughter.

Why was everything so funny when they were together? It was irritating. The inside jokes could only lead to trouble. I don't think it was a jealousy, but rather, knowing how vulnerable Hannah was and my feeling concerned Jean was venturing into areas that needed professional help, not anecdotal prescriptive truths from the busybody next door.

Ricky's tidbit about their son, though. That was something to ponder on. I'd been so thrown off by the burner phone altercation with Hannah, I hadn't given it a lot of thought.

If my goal was to be her protector, was I failing? Or just overreacting?

It wasn't my place to control her, but if I stepped back too far, she might end up in dire straits. I went in the front door, engaging more with Jean. I walked toward the coffee pot and poured myself a cup.

"Well, I guess it just makes sense for me to come hang out, too," I said. "I could use a good laugh."

The tone of the conversation changed between the two of them upon my arrival. I wasn't the guy to want to know every detail of my wife's day, nor her every conversation or message, but I didn't enjoy feeling out of the loop, either. It was a balancing act — unfair to crowd, but not right to neglect. You know, that fine line of caring too little or too much.

I sat down.

"Well? What's up?" I asked, noticing a couple of our high school yearbooks on the table.

Jean smiled. "I saw that incredibly gelled hair you *used* to have, and I found out Hannah was a homecoming queen. You've got a good thing going for you, Benjamin Decker."

"How about you? Were you a homecoming queen?" I asked.

"No. I never fit the bill. I think it was the hair. Yeah, it must have been."

Hannah kicked at my leg.

Jean stood up. "I was just leaving as you pulled in. I... uh, I'll see you later."

"Okay. Alright, we'll go with that. Hope your shift goes well."

"You're the only shifty one here, Benjamin. Thanks for the coffee, darlin'," she said, walking out the front door. She scurried toward the Roadmaster, its backfire telling the whole block she was on the way out.

"She's going east," I mumbled to Hannah as I sipped my coffee.

"Why do you care? Is this some game for you?"

"No. I just find it annoying she won't tell us."

"I've had enough chats with her at this point to know whatever it is isn't all that interesting or fulfilling. It's just a job, Ben. If it were something exhilarating or involved dancing naked around a pole, she wouldn't whine so much about policies and paperwork."

"Are you kidding? I bet I got more out of her in that little thirty second conversation than you have in days."

"Well, way to go, Mr. Interrogator. Or should I say intimidator? I was finally getting her to open up and you barge in! Don't turn this into a competition," she said.

"Hannah, Hannah," I said, reaching out for her hand. She pulled away.

"I won't let you control me anymore."

I scoffed. "Control you?"

"You just want to twist me into your delusions and keep me on your terms and conditions."

"You've got to be kidding. Where's this coming from?"

"Am I kidding?" she asked.

"This just seems out of left field."

"So do you. I don't know if I can even trust you anymore."

"What? What the hell are you saying?" I asked, my nostrils flaring.

"Go look in our bedroom. I tucked it under your pillow."

I stood up, charging that way.

"A subscription to LadyLove Magazine?" I yelled. "Are you kidding me?"

"Yeah. I guess that's enough for you. And to have the gall to just have it mailed here, with your name on it? Davey checked the mail earlier, asshat. Thank God they had it in that black protective sleeve."

I picked up the magazine and thumbed through it, nodding my head and smirking. Lots of shapes, curves, and bizarre angles with cheap lighting and photography. A collapsing byproduct of an era fading away into something new — not any better, just modern.

I scoffed, throwing it in the trash. "This crap isn't mine. I wouldn't do that to you. Besides, who orders a subscription to something like this these days? It's newsstand riffraff, and with the internet the way it is, I mean, come on!"

"Between the burner phone and the filthy magazine, I'm scared to find out what's next."

"Hannah, you're not buying into this, are you? It's just a college roommate pulling a prank."

"At $10.95 an issue for twelve months? That's pricey."

"I'm just saying, most men would go elsewhere before they had that shipped to their house."

"Well, what are you going to do with it?" she asked.

"You can't just throw it away. That's every teenager's dream to find one of those."

"Well, what do you suggest, dreamer?"

"Your dad's kind of old school. We'll give it to him."

"Great. There's a mental image I could have lived without seeing. My 73-year-old father with a stack of LadyLove and... whatever."

"Maybe we can call the magazine and figure out who's behind this, because it's not me!"

"Jean and I already tried. They wouldn't give us the information. Said it's confidential."

"Jean knows about this? That's none of her damn business. Is it?" I said, slamming my fist down. "This is between us and whatever idiot subscribed us."

"Whatever you say, controlling me again..."

"Let's go back to the call. Did you *really* stiff arm them?"

"Yeah. It was no use. I even used my mom voice."

I tried to hug her to ease up the mood. Her cold glare reassured me it was useless.

I figured I'd lay it all out there while tempers were hot. "I'm just not feeling good about the amount of time you're spending with Jean lately. You haven't picked up a paintbrush in days. Are you inviting her over or is she just showing up?"

She sighed. "I get home from picking up Davey. She's outside watering the dirt."

I interrupted. "The thing is... you have to seed it before you water it."

Hannah glared at me. "She's watering... we wave. And then, one thing leads to another. It seems normal. You know, what friends do? You'd know that better... if you had any."

I shook my head. I was guilty of keeping most people in the acquaintance zone because of trust issues I'd rather not dwell upon. "Well, maybe tomorrow, just break up the routine a little. Park on the side street. Go in the back door."

"Why?" she asked.

"I just want to know what her goal is with us."

"Not everyone has an ulterior motive. Can't you get that?"

"I do get that, and I'm telling you right now, this woman has one. Do it for me. Just this once. Break the pattern and see how she acts."

"Just being honest with you, Ben, you're sounding half a step from crazy right now."

"When it comes to keeping you and Davey safe, I hope my commitment means something."

"Safe? What's so unsafe about a cup of coffee with a neighbor?"

"Hannah, it's not just any neighbor. There's something about... Jean."

"You're full of it. I think it's about time we get you some help for your own good. Why don't you go spend some time outside? I hear our son's looking for a dad."

I stormed out.

# ON PARENTS

A parent's bond with their child is hard to describe. It's fluid. It's pliable. And it can get downright ugly in a matter of minutes — sometimes seconds.

Dad never did much to bond with me until I came of age, at least, not from a developmental sort of perspective. I would get myself into trouble meddling in my parents' personal affairs, interjecting myself into their arguments and, sometimes, siding with whichever one might have been my favorite for a given week, which often changed depending on their alcohol consumption.

Life was hard. Money was tight. And I was always stuck with the leftovers. I'm not saying in retrospect I don't feel for my parents or that my father was unjustified in the occasional ass whipping he'd give. I just resented him more with time.

It would be easy to misunderstand. Years later and with him long gone, there's just nothing to salvage. Just scraps and pieces of me left here or there. I suppose it's only natural for one to consider ways to cope with these kinds of problems. Maybe therapy, booze, medicine, but for me, it's always been about escape — going somewhere I've never been and hiding a while. I guess that's what Dad did. There was no clean ending for us. No closure.

***

I talked with Davey for a few minutes, throwing the ball with him. We reminisced about Jake. And as I warmed him up to visit more, I figured he might have more to say.

"What do you think about Miss Jean?"

"She's Mommy's new friend."

"Yeah. It seems like she's been over a lot lately. Is that bothering you?"

"No."

I caught myself doing something I promised I never would. It wasn't fair to any of us.

"You don't want your mommy to spend more time with you?"

Davey shook his head. "I don't know. I guess so," he said, throwing the ball back to me.

"Miss Jean is nice to Mommy."

"What do you mean... nice?"

"She listens to her."

"What's that supposed to mean?"

"Mommy told Miss Jean you don't listen well, you interrupt, and make conversations all about you."

"She did? And you heard all of that? Are you sure?"

"Mommy didn't know I was listening. I was in my room with my ear up to the door. Miss Jean told her a new way to be happy."

"What was that?"

"I don't know. I couldn't hear. They just kept laughing. I came out of my room and went back outside."

I abused my power again. "Well, I just want to keep Mommy safe. Let's make sure we watch out for her. If Miss Jean stays around too long, you can go in and interrupt. You deserve time with your mommy, too. Don't tell her I told you that, though."

"Why, Daddy? Secrets don't make friends."

"What *do* they do?" I asked.

"They make people evil."

"Doesn't everyone have secrets?"

"Grown-ups do. And some grown-ups have lots of secrets. Like you, Daddy!" he said.

"What are you talking about?"

"There are a lot of hours in your day we don't know about."

"We?"

"Me and Mommy."

"Does Mommy say that to you?"

"I don't know."

"What?"

"I don't know."

I grabbed him by the arm. "I need to know. Where are you hearing that? From Mommy?"

"I don't remember."

"Well, someone is telling you these things, Davey. You have to remember."

"I don't. I think it was just a dream I had."

"You know what I've told you about dreams. They're just your imagination, son," I said.

"But sometimes they're true, Daddy."

"You're right, bud. Sometimes they are."

## DRIFTING

I awoke alone. A creaking sound caught my attention. I stood up and stepped into the bathroom, splashing some water on my face. I heard the noise again and walked into the hallway to check. A streak of red lined the floor going toward Hannah's back bedroom studio. Hannah was painting. I contemplated going in, planning out a script to follow, something to ease our discord, but couldn't find it. Every way I played out the scenario in my head, it ended poorly. Not even Pat Bateman was this cracked.

Eventually, Jean's voice arrived.

*Fate stole him away too soon. Or was it that little blue pill? Liar! Liar! Liar!*

Her cackling laugh pushed me to knock on the door.

Simple Plan played on the stereo. I let myself in. The canvas was opposite me, so I couldn't see it.

"Hey. Are you free for a visitor?"

She looked at me, zoning back in on her painting. If she nodded, it was so weak a nod, I didn't see. There was also no head shake. Though I wasn't in the oust zone, I loitered close.

"How's it coming?" I asked.

She turned the painting around. The backdrop was predominantly red across the canvas. 1739 was slightly out of focus while demons hovered in the foreground somewhere in the driveway between our houses, her silhouette standing in the kitchen window looking toward us.

"Do you want to talk about it?"

She shook her head.

"Do you want me to talk about it?" I asked.

"I want you to shut up and let me paint."

"It's 2AM. We've got to get to bed."

"I'm on a tear, Ben. Let me do my thing. I'll be in there in a while."

I must have drifted an hour or two, but when I woke, Hannah was next to me in bed. I wrapped my arm around her.

"Stop!" she said, flinging it off and rolling over.

# EX MARKS THE SPOT

I remembered my meeting with Ricky scheduled that night. Maybe I could get some answers about Jean. I arrived at IronWorks. It was a smaller world than I could have realized. The balding man from the grief support group was sitting at the bar. It was Ricky. I knew he'd recognize me, but I also never told anyone in the group my name. There was an unspoken anonymity in the meetings. It was up to us when we reveal this kind of thing, and Hannah and I opted to err on the side of caution in case of deranged psychos attending the group.

"Ricky?"

"Will?"

"Guilty as charged," I said, shaking hands with him. "What are the odds? Let me buy your next round."

"I won't argue."

Ricky may have already had a few too many because he didn't ask about why Hannah and I stopped attending the group. The answer boiled down to my conclusion it did more harm than good. I brought it up anyway.

"So, group therapy? I didn't realize we knew each other from there," I said.

"I guess so."

"Yeah, support group. You lost your son... and then your wife?"

"Yeah, I did everything I could to hang on, but it was never enough. That car crash was just too far out of control."

"Car crash?"

"My old lady, her noggin was riddled with thoughts, man. The crap that haunts your dreams... I'm sorry."

"It's okay. I'm the one who asked."

I guess the alcohol had him loose.

"Yeah. I go to the group for different reasons. Sure, we lost our kid, and that broke my heart, but he was a drug addict. Those damn Garashock pills. No parent wants to admit it, but that's costly. So, we missed him... Jeanie especially, but I guess I saw things a little differently. That added to the drama. There were just things that happened, man. Things I can't hardly say," he said, sipping his drink. "I don't think you're the one to tell this to. You're trying to sell the place, right? Some kind of realtor?"

"Yeah," I said. "I've got a thirty-something family interested. I'm just trying to get some context on the lay of the land."

Ricky scratched his chin, gulping down another pint of the house beer on tap. "Well, that's loaded, man."

"What do you mean?"

"About twenty years ago, half that block belonged to Jean's family. She's the only one left now. If it sounds hard to fathom, it's because it is."

I shook my head. "They all just up and moved on?"

"She did it to 'em."

"Huh?"

"It was just her games, man. The kind of thing you expect busybodies to do."

"And, forgive my saying this, if it annoyed you so much, why'd you put up with it?"

"She's a master manipulator. She always follows a pattern. It's not predictable, but it's the same semantics, over and over. I had to get out to realize that."

"You're saying she's crazy?"

He shook his head. "I'm saying she's beyond that. She's got like... full blown... issues."

I worked on my first pint. "Like what?"

"She gets set off by something and starts playing out the craziest things in her head, man. And then it fades away again. That's why I told the people in group about the CSD."

"I wondered about that before."

"It might sound stupid, but it was just a moniker I coined in therapy called Crazy Spouse Disorder. I bet it's even worse now, like an empty-nester phenomenon. I grieve it every day because her antics uh... they got me into trouble, too. I'm sorry. I'm here to talk to you about the house."

"Go on, then."

"Her mom, she lived there for her last five years or so. I felt sorry for her. I never knew what to do."

"What do you mean?"

"She'd always go on and on like there was a lot wrong with her mother, insisting she needed doctors and checkups, that the dementia was overtaking her, and that she needed constant care, but refused getting a professional diagnosis — hers was good enough because she had a degree in *Dr. Oz*."

I chuckled. "Well, he's... uh... certainly something, but personally, I'd prefer a degree in *Dr. Phil*."

"Well, she's got one of those too, man!"

"Damn."

Ricky shook his head, his eyes looking somewhere above my head at some women shooting billiards at the table behind us. "I'm rambling. I never saw a diagnosis in writing. And anytime I challenged it, she all but bit my nose off and I mean that in the most literal sense."

"Why didn't you go to the police?"

"I screwed up, too."

"How's that?"

"I've had too many beers. I got to go. The house is fine. You just need to make sure you watch your back around Jean. She's just one of them... bad news bears."

"Great flick," I said.

"I hated it."

"Take care, Ricky. I'll get the tab."

"You're too kind, man. I'll get you another time. Maybe I'll see you at group again?"

"Maybe."

"One more question, Ricky. Jean's mother, did she live in one of the front bedrooms or the back one?"

"It was always the back one."

I had no words as sickness overtook me. An inexplicable vision had told me so. We locked eyes, and I felt as if he sensed it. Ricky excused himself. I wondered how much of our heart-to-heart would be recalled the next day and contemplated how I might use the information.

Truth was, all it would take was a drive by for Ricky to find me and my family and mess us up if he wanted to, but something told me Jean's scar was not one to revisit. I mean, there's always a chance you get your throat slit in your sleep. Would it be any more satisfying if it was someone you know? I was wrong to mislead him, but I needed something to ground me. Someone rational that wasn't in the middle of the mess I was caught up in. Ricky may have been that man a year ago, but he was out, and at that moment, that seemed safer.

I guess I lost track of time. One beer led to two, then three, and then I lost count. As friendly as the bartender was, we wasted the night away talking sports, politics, and failed movie sequels. Better yet, I scored a new client for Garashock. So, all in all, it wasn't a wasted trip. I'd left my phone in the car that night. Unreachable was better. As my eyes met the clock above the bar next to the TV with *SportsCenter* screen burn, the bar closed down.

I found my way to the Mercedes, too wasted to drive, so I just collapsed in there for a while. No calls or texts to return. Hannah wasn't looking for me yet, so I'd just sleep it off and tell her I was working late again.

# ADVICE

Things weren't stacking up well. I don't know if I was on an island or if Hannah was, but we'd drifted further than we should. I let work get in the way. As basic as this might sound to the average working-class family with kids, there was nothing simple about our problems. There were layers. And though I couldn't work my way through every one of them, it seemed appropriate to piece together a strategy for improving our situation.

I ran into Mori at the water cooler. It was too convenient a place for chit-chat, so I invited him to my office. A subordinate taking initiative this way wasn't out of place, Mori was just that approachable. He empowered us, and preferred it when we took initiative, often waiting for us to make the first move. Though that was a stretch at times, I needed regular reinforcement to keep the fire lit.

"What is it?" he asked, his hand resting under his chin.

"I'm struggling, Mori."

"I know. I see it. You're short on sleep. Your shirt's not pressed. Your breath reeks."

I sighed. "Yeah."

"It shows a lot. When you're ready, tell me what's going on and we take care of it."

"What?"

"I said, we take care of it."

"Mori... Mori... what does that mean?"

"No more questions. Olkovs take care of our own."

He walked out of the room. It wasn't guilt or remorse I was feeling at the moment. It was fear. Ultimately, mind games were Mori's approach to this kind of situation. I pulled my desk drawer open as a headache came over me and took a loose aspirin next to the paperclips. I couldn't focus. Any time I tried, Jean parked herself in my brain.

*Oh Benny, Ben. You know you're interfering with your wife's order. You're adding to the chaos. And here I am trying to be the good neighbor she needs, and you can't do anything but fuss. Ben Decker, you need some help, and I don't know what else to do for you.*

I worked to bury the feeling, but somehow in that moment, I could only revisit that day in her living room, the *Jerry Springer* rerun on full blast. The look in Hannah's eyes. That feeling of our intrusion.

How could she have pivoted from so crazy to so normal in such a short amount of time?

Was I delusional?

Had we caught her at her worst that day?

Was I slipping away?

I refused to accept it. There was more. There had to be. And I had to figure out why. That's when her voice overtook my brain again.

*You want to know me, don't you? You need to find me. You miss me. You feel you're on the edge of a cliff and just waiting for it to bottom out, don't you? Oh, Benjamin, my Benjamin, your obsession is cute. It's normal. And I welcome you.*

I looked at the Garashock 500s on my desk. I wondered why Olkov wasn't shuttered. The gravity of our business. The television in my office was playing *Wall Street*.

Gordon Gekko - *"Greed, for lack of a better word, is good."*

"Yeah... right, Gordo," I muttered.

Olkov produced more and more, and the bottom line was as profitable as I'd ever seen. Mori just bought his way out, I guess. I wasn't ready for legal ramifications, nor was I prepared if they arrived. We were being watched, and I pondered the depths of the repercussions.

A few minutes after an uneventful lunch, aside from an awkward conversation with Bob Dowdy in the breakroom about hair plug maintenance, there was little worth mentioning. I skipped past Mori's assistant and into his office.

"You have a minute?"

"For you, my friend, two." he said, motioning toward the seat across from his desk. His office was nothing flashy. It was unassuming for a chief executive, but that was Mori. He dressed the part and had the car, but carried himself as an everyman in conversations, and perhaps that was the ticket to his recurring success.

"Mori, there's someone in my life that is interrupting me, and my family. And..."

"And?"

"And I don't know what to do."

Mori snapped his fingers. "Details. I need details," he said, pulling out a bottle of scotch from his desk drawer into two glasses.

"There's a woman."

"Oooh."

"No. No. Not like that."

"It's my neighbor."

"Even more spicy," he said, his accent thick as always.

"It's not a romantic thing, Mori. It's a personal matter between my wife and I."

"Why you bring your troubles to work? Leave work at work, home at home. This is junior analyst 101, not for executives."

"I don't know what else to do?"

"Call your father."

"He's dead."

"Your mother."

"She doesn't answer my calls anymore."

"And why is that, Ben?"

"She and Hannah... they don't get along."

"Well, even Russians appreciate Hitchcock. Hmm-hmm," he said, smiling. "I know you appreciate that!"

"What?"

"Boy's best friend is..."

"His mother. Vernon Dalhart wrote a song with that phrase long before it was a line in a book or a movie."

"Yes, Ben, but no one cares."

"What changed between you and your mother?"

"Hannah."

"No blaming, Ben. You changed."

"I disagree. I like to be consistent, predictable, dependable. That's Ben Decker."

"Leave and cleave," he said, sipping his scotch.

"What?"

"Leave your mother, cleave your wife."

"Mori, you're not making any sense. I thought you just said the opposite."

"Key word before was boy. You are no boy, Ben. You are married man. It's time to act like one."

"I feel like this is getting me nowhere, Mori. I mean no disrespect, but my fuse is short."

He pulled out a cigar. "Money buys happiness. Anyone telling you otherwise... full of shit," he said, swiping both of his hands against one another and lighting it up.

"So?"

"So, you need to get neighbor out of life. What have you tried?"

"Not much. She and my wife seem like they're best friends already."

"Oh, Ben, are you jealous type? Need more 'me and you' time? Tsk-tsk."

"Mori, I'm serious. I think this woman is dangerous. And I feel like she's always watching."

"Why? How is she dangerous?"

"It's a hunch."

"Like Notre Dame? That hunch?"

"No. Like a gut instinct. I know something is off."

He nodded. "Okay, I see. Maybe you send message indirectly."

"Any ideas?"

"We host party your house. Nice big party. Olkov dime. We invite few other friends, maybe some neighbors you don't know, and then, we skip neighbor."

"Mori, you're forgetting something here, my wife. She'll try to invite the neighbor, so she doesn't feel left out."

"Ben, Ben, tell your wife the plan."

"But she's not gonna be in favor of the plan, Mori. That's the whole problem. I'm just the 'controlling' spouse."

"Are you?" he asked.

I shook my head. "Of course not."

"Okay, then. Well, you figure out way. Get creative. Tell red lie."

"A what? A red lie? Don't you mean, white lie?"

"No. No. Red lie... it's spite and revenge."

"Whoa there. I'm not sure I'm to the spiting phase yet."

"Okay, then tell white lie. If she's that close, she'll lose her hots when she sees your wife host big party without help or input, right?"

"Lose her cool. I don't know, Mori. This seems harsh."

"She needs to know it's happening, she's not invited, and it's no private event. She's off list, Ben.

"Mori, you're forgetting that I live next to this woman. The aftermath..."

"It's mind games, Ben. You need hand on top."

"Upper hand."

"Yes, right. Hmm-hmm."

"Alright. Let me put some thought into it. So, you're telling me to just invite the regional team, some neighbor friends, and put it all on the company dime?"

"Yes. I need people well. This is eating your insides. We must fix."

"Thanks, Mori."

"Don't waste time. I sense it, Ben. You need to make life better. I want that for my best workers."

# MELTDOWN

They say a good neighbor's hard to come by, and whoever they might be, are mostly right.

I contemplated Mori's proposal awhile, and it donned on me my investigation into Miss Jean could go further. My mood mellowed, and I had purpose again. As unstable as I'd felt, the chat with Mori was good. I don't recommend therapy with your boss. It can get sloppy quickly, but in my moment of desperation, the unorthodox idea from Mori seemed perfect. As I drove home that afternoon, I thought about how to present it to Hannah. There was no way I could win.

I pulled into the driveway after a quick stop for hamburgers. I noticed Jean's car outside 1739. Davey was in the yard kicking his soccer ball and Gonzo relieved himself behind the Crape Myrtle out front.

"Come on!" I yelled, raising my hands at the pup.

"Daddy, you're home!" Davey said, running toward me.

I hugged him.

"What's going on, bud?"

"Not too much. Mom's having me practice for soccer. I think I want to play."

"Oh, yeah?"

"Yeah. I'm thinking about it. A few of the other kids are."

"Alright! Well, what's this guy doing in our yard?" I bent down and pet Gonzo. "Got more fleas to hop around in my grass?"

"No. He's just playing with me. Mommy and Miss Jean are out back having coffee. They asked if I would watch him."

"And they just left you out here all by yourself in the front yard?"

"They said it would only be a few minutes."

"Well, let's go check on them. You can bring your ball and play out back, too."

"Okay, Dad."

I stopped for a minute when I went inside. I was growing more and more concerned with Hannah's judgment. She was floating adrift, and I didn't know how to help. I froze up, staring out the window and somehow, in that moment, the ugly vines and drooping vents that once graced Jean's house looked manicured and cleaned up. The junk in the yard was gone, and I was losing it. She couldn't have picked up all of that so quickly.

Jean's voice was loud and proud.

*No... no... Benjamin... you can't clean it up.*

I covered my ears, clenching my eyes shut a second. I looked out again. The house was trashed. I convinced myself the demons Hannah painted were in the driveway a second before they disappeared.

"Are you okay, Dad?" Davey asked.

"I don't know, bud."

I worked my way to the back, my heart rate escalating as Davey went to his room. Hannah and Jean were sitting on the back patio furniture laughing the afternoon away, more and more coffee to entertain. I stepped outside.

"And that's when Ben finally broke down and admitted to me he ate the entire package," Hannah said, grinning.

"Ha-ha-ha!" Jean laughed coarsely. She looked up at me and stopped, her eyes shifting toward Hannah.

"What's this about?" I asked.

"Your wife, Ben, she's something else. I bet she could have a stand-up act — mostly at your expense!"

Hannah's look told me another story.

"How are you?" I said, leaning in to kiss her. She pulled away.

"What's wrong?" I asked.

"You tell me what's wrong, Ben. How was lunch?"

"Fine. I got a taco from the drive through... went back to the office... finished some call reports... had a chat with Mori."

"Are you sure?"

"Yes. Very sure."

"We'll talk about this more later."

"No," I said. "This is awkward, but if you're going to air something out on the laundry line behind my back, let's get this done, here and now."

She sighed. "Tina."

"Who?"

"Tina Monroe. You met her at Fratelli's earlier, didn't you?"

"What the hell are you talking about? Tina Monroe, as in high school girlfriend, Tina? Are you kidding me?"

"Ben, she messaged me earlier. I know about DateMeHoney."

"What?!"

"Come on, Ben!" Hannah said, handing me some print outs. There was a photo of me from the internet on a profile. She read it aloud. "Ben Decker. 36. Single. Dad. Looking for a cute mommy to play house with. I sell pharmaceuticals and make a lot more than mine or yours ever did. Take a ride in my Mercedes if you want, and we'll get acquainted. 14 hearts, 3 likes, and a 5 date requests within fifty miles..."

I scoffed. "Hannah, I didn't write that!"

Hannah continued, her voice deepening to imitate mine. "Hey sweetheart. I know it's been years. I can't get you off my mind. I miss you."

I shook my head. "This is ridiculous."

Hannah's voice became higher pitched. "Oh my gosh, Ben Decker. What's it been? Nineteen years?"

"Hannah!" I looked over at Jean. Her flat grin and wide eyes told me she was there to protect.

Hannah's voice became deeper again. "I've had a lot of time to think. Maybe we can grab a coffee or lunch at Fratelli's?"

I sighed, dropping my head into my hands.

High-pitched Hannah. "Aren't you married with kids?"

"Come on!" I yelled.

"Read the next part."

"No!"

"Read it!"

"I didn't write this!" I said.

"Read it, now!" she said, slapping me across the face.

I gave in. "She's a cheating bitch! My kid deserves better." I chunked the paper on the ground.

"Don't forget this one," she said, putting it right in my face. "BenDeckerDad@gmail.com!"

There was a slew of e-mails back and forth — Profiles setup on different sites and accounts, mostly of the offensive and inappropriate type.

I looked over at Jean and then back at Hannah. Their arms were crossed. "It's not how it looks. This is some kind of setup."

"Oh, Benjamin," Jean said, "sing your song and let Hannah sing hers."

"I swear on my father's grave. I don't do online dating."

"So, you're telling me that someone's impersonating you online now, too?" Hannah said. "How would they know about Tina?"

"I don't know."

I kept thinking the conversation would get tense enough that Jean would leave, but she didn't.

"I guess you're the mother hen, now? Looking out for her, huh?" I grumbled.

"Treat her better and I wouldn't have to!" Jean said, slamming her coffee cup on the table. "Man up!"

Hannah hurled a checkbook at me.

*Hannah Weller (Personal Account)*
*First National Bank*

"Weller? Personal account? What the hell is this?"

"A little insurance policy," Jean said. "I told Hannah the separate bank account would be a good first step. I even floated her an account opening deposit."

"Hannah, you just went along with this?"

Hannah sighed. "Ben, I don't know who you are anymore. You're disappearing randomly... not coming home at night... the burner phone... the magazines... after Jean showed me all this with Tina, we had to do something to send a message."

"We... or you?"

Hannah looked away. I looked over at Jean as she dropped her eyebrows.

I was ready to snap her like a twig, so I walked it off and went into the garage. I had a little mini-fridge with some stubby beer bottles. I popped one open and pulled the door closed. The blue camping chair sufficed to sulk. Hannah wouldn't come in anytime soon and neither would Davey. At some point, maybe you'd have a shred of regret for storming off, but I just didn't. I hated being wronged this way. I didn't want to come out.

Jean's voice butted into my musings.

*Dumb. Dumb. Dumb. That's all you are, Benjamin. The tango isn't so fun anymore, is it? That ugly truth right in front of her!*

After a few hours of nothing but booze, anger, and confusion, I went inside and found my way to the bedroom. Hannah was on our bed watching a *Golden Girls* rerun while she sketched an idea for a new painting.

"About earlier..." I said, trailing off.

I hoped she would chime in. She kept sketching. The drawing looked like more demons, this time circling around me, flames behind my eyes.

"Aren't you going to hear me out?"

She sighed. "What about it? That I caught you red-handed?"

I shook my head. "Check my phone. Whatever computer you want. I swear to you. You know I'm not the swearing type. I didn't do that."

"Well, Ben, it's awfully convenient to lie sometimes, isn't it? Didn't you say that in a sales pitch once? Use it to work your angle?"

"Hannah, this is stupid," I said, standing up and pacing the room.

"You're about the right age for a breakdown," she said. "You could have just slipped a few times and screwed up. If you would own that, I might be more understanding, but doing everything in your power to lie about it, Ben. That *irks* me."

"I'm not lying," I yelled, slamming my fist into the wall and denting the sheetrock. "I'm sorry. I..."

"Prove it!" she said.

"You've got to distance yourself from this... friend. What kind of person just sits there and watches that kind of argument, enables that kind of behavior? Does that not ring any alarm bells? Red flags? Wouldn't most normal people want to leave and let the other parties duke it out? She doesn't care about you, Hannah."

"You're just trying to drive a wedge between us."

"I'm sure that's exactly what she told you. That I'm the bad guy. That *I'm* the damn abuser! That's bullshit and you know it!"

"You've got to get yourself together, Ben. If Davey and I can't trust you, there's no point, anymore."

I slept little that night. I wanted to know why Hannah rushed so quickly to believing there wasn't something farfetched about most of this behavior. My track record was tried and true. I'd never cheat. I just needed to prove it.

# BANG!

I woke early and left before Hannah and Davey were up. That seemed the best strategy. Darting across town to the east side, I stopped by the pawn shop near the bedsheet plant. I'd been giving this guy, Rocko, 500s in my nighttime wanderings regularly to keep a revolving door of knock off Rolexes at my disposal. You know, to swap out in the moments I felt my real ones were threatened.

As for the shop, it was dated, grody, and slimy. There was just something about the place that lured me. The stories behind the random trinkets people would bring in. I'm sure Rocko had plenty. My eyes always met the gun rack on the back wall behind the counter. I'd never relented, but they beckoned from behind the glass.

"Rocko, man, I need a gun."

"A gun... what for, Ben?"

"Protection."

Rocko nodded, taking the jeweler's eye magnifier off his head and looking at me. "Are you alright?"

"I'm good. A little short on sleep. I've got to get a few transactions in flight today to keep the boss man happy."

"Alright," he said. "You don't need anything big and flashy for your gateway gun."

"What's wrong with a .44 Magnum?"

"Your head. It'll blow clean off," he said, mimicking Clint Eastwood. "Take this ditty. It's a Russian import — Saturday Night Special."

"Alright. I'll go with that. Discrete is good. If my old lady spotted this, she'd string me up and splatter me."

"Ha. Benny, old buddy, it won't bother you that the serial number is filed off, will it?"

"Works for me," I said. He rang me up, smudging some paperwork for delayed processing and I was on my way out.

I loaded up on some samples from the back of the bedsheet plant and started making my rounds through town before eventually getting back to West Side.

Just across the lot from the Denny's next door sat a state facility, home to a bunch of health and human service departments often forgotten. I drove by. A wood-paneled Roadmaster was parked out front in one of the employee parking spots. The building featured no law enforcement presence, only bureaucratic and social worker types. I was sure it was Jean's.

I didn't know if it was a relief or a disappointment. I mean, Jean Jackson didn't strike me as FBI material, nor DEA, not even a rent-a-cop, but somehow, I'd hoped her choice to withhold her job meant she did something more interesting than filling out food stamp forms.

I found my way into the building. The lobby was full of single mothers, malnourished children, and deadbeat dads desperate for a shave and a haircut. I approached the lobby counter, overdressed for my surroundings, but looking more and more the part, all things considered.

The woman behind the glass didn't acknowledge me, so I spoke up.

"Ma'am, I'd like a word when you have a second."

She continued to focus on whatever had her attention. So typical. There was a little sign on the table that said *Ring Bell for Service.*

I spoke up again. "Ma'am, do you have a moment?" When she didn't reply that time, I sighed loudly.

I rang the bell, and she looked up. "How can I help you?"

"You could start by acknowledging when I say hello."

"Touchy. Touchy," she said, slamming her rubber stamp on some paperwork.

"Listen, I'm here to see a friend. I was hoping to catch her on her lunch hour. Maybe you could give her a nudge?"

"What department?"

"Oh... uh... I don't know. Food stamps?"

"Name?"

"Jean Jackson."

"Negative."

"Women Infants Children."

"Nope."

"Family and Protective Services."

"Nada."

"What other departments do you have buried in here?"

"What kind of friend doesn't know where their 'friend' works? What's your name?"

I shook my head. "I'm sorry. I guess I better go. You're wasting my time, and I guess I'm wasting yours."

"Wait, sir! I can pass on a message or let her know you stopped by."

"Not necessary. I'll catch up with her another time."

What was I doing? I climbed back in the car and moved toward the expressway. Every radio station was on a commercial break, and I heard her voice again.

*What was that all about, Benjamin? You want what you can't have? Why?*

Break was over. I turned the radio up louder, hoping to drown her out. "Piano Man" by Billy Joel came through the speakers.

A police car pulled up behind me, and I panicked. My gun was in my jacket pocket. No serial number. The officer must have been running my plates. I wasn't a stalker. I had a trunk full of medicine and I'd put off that car inspection a month too long, but honestly, there was bound to be someone else around here that needed stopping more than me. I was sure of it. I was just in the neighborhood. Maybe going inside the building was a step too far. I couldn't be the nut. I left abruptly from the facility but harassed no one. I wondered if my description would get back to Jean, though. And if it did, maybe I shouldn't be all that bothered. It would just send a message that I was onto her.

Just as I pulled out my registration from the glove box, the officer scooted ahead faster than I expected.

I went through my day, stopping by the usual drop-off points and raking in a few sales on the Garashock 500 pills. I drove past Suit Warehouse Direct and turned around to pull in. How upscale an operation was it? I approached the door, and the salesperson greeted me. My jacket was looking worse for wear. So, I figured what the hay, why not go for the blue jacket special?

"Yeah, I'm looking for a new blazer. I was hoping for something in navy."

"Oh, okay," the man said, slowly, the little ruler dangling from his neck. "Something navy?"

"Yeah. Any... blue jacket specials?"

He sized me up a few times with the measurements. "Yeah, you're a 42 long. I think I've got one in the back that looks like this one on display. Why don't I grab it for you and see what you think?"

"Works for me."

The salesman came back with the jacket. The front pocket looked puffed. I put it on and eyed it in the mirror.

"Looks great," he said. "They normally run $299, but considering the... alterations, it's $349. Is that okay?"

I nodded. "Buddy, I'm in sales. Never ask if it's okay. Just say it. Take it or leave it. There shouldn't seem like there's room to negotiate."

"So?"

"So, I'll take it."

"Let's ring you up. Our tailor's on the go most of the time, but we do... alterations the third Wednesday of every month, so if you ever need anything... addressed, we're here. We'll make sure you like the way you look. That's a guarantee!"

"Guarantee, huh? Did you rip that off?"

I swiped my card and took my jacket. Stepping outside, I spotted a man with a poorly coiffed bird's nest on top of his head, fumbling for his keys in the car next to mine.

"Hey," he said.

"Hi."

"I know I may not be the best-looking ambulance chaser you've ever seen, but I watch guys like you come into Suit Warehouse Direct all the time and give out my card. Joe Levens, Attorney."

"Nice to meet you, Joe. What makes you think I need one?"

"The food containers in the back of your car. The stain on your pants. Your unshaven face. Your crooked glasses. Your flustered demeanor. You look like you're on the path to the big D, my friend."

"Oh?" I said.

"Too honest?"

"No. I'll take honesty any day, Joe. There's not enough of it."

We shook hands, and I went on my way.

I scooted across town to the office. I hadn't reached in to check my pocket until that point. Sure enough, that extra fifty-bucks scored me a twelve pack of Garashock 500s. Our incredible supply chain at work.

# BACON AND EGGS

I went straight to work the next morning, proceeding toward the motel distribution center. I wondered about Jean. I was still fixated. Why did I care?

I mean, should we be that concerned about our next-door neighbor's employer? I guess it all depends on who you ask. Some might say it's a stretch. Others would find themselves right at home knowing that neighbor Bob, Tom, or Jean, in this case, worked down at the dairy farm. What kind of people did their trade attract? Are they coming by the house at all hours? Are they the type that might carry over or bleed into your lifestyle? These are all just food for thought.

How many times do we ask someone what they do when we're working our way down the chit-chat list? Maybe there's a few of us that actually want to vet the person we're talking to — to understand the trade or to prepare for the worst-case scenario. Most of the time, it's a non-issue. Just a throwaway sort of question, but maybe when you find out your neighbor owns a bar, runs a strip club, or manages hedge funds, you might have a little more to be concerned about. It's all a matter of association. It was stupid not to ask before. I'd been with her ex, having it all spoon-fed to me, essentially. There was a guilt about me. I knew if I spent too much time around Ricky, I would feel emotionally invested. That's a path that may or may not be all that pertinent to me or to you. Then again, there's a context, a color to it. Of course, I suppose that's where the struggle for one in such a situation occurs.

My mind raced fifty-four directions. I was aimless.

I arrived at the motel. The Denny's next door was a police hangout, but they'd never bothered us. Jean was watching me. The Roadmaster was parked outside under a pecan tree. The color scheme, the bird crap and tree sap, it looked like Jean's. It must have been.

I'd never been serious enough to truly consider myself under surveillance. That was all just a bunch of nerves because most of us aren't that important, not even close. Now, was there any chance she was just there to have her breakfast and coincidentally me be there? It seemed she worked next door, but I didn't believe she would eat there. This was easily the ugliest location in town and if a roach egg wasn't also gracing your plate of poached eggs, you were lucky, and I mean that in the sincerest of ways.

I thought I could make out Jean's silhouette in the restaurant's window facing the motel. I decided to go over there and grab a cup of coffee. Maybe we'd have a run in. I came in, found my way to the back corner booth where I'd spotted her through the window.

I sat down. "This can't be right, Jeanie," I said.

"What are you doing here? Are *you* following me?" she asked.

"I don't know what you mean."

"I think you do!" I said, grabbing a bacon strip from her plate and eating it. "You just got a little bored, followed me to work, and convinced yourself watching me could fulfill those unmet needs of yours. It must be a lonely life."

Jean started looking around the restaurant, making note of witnesses. "Benjamin, this isn't what we..."

I continued my tirade. "Is that okay with you? Is that okay with you, Jean? Homewrecker! This woman's a damn homewrecker! Watch out, people. She could be after you next."

Jean looked at me, pulling away.

"Jean Jackson!" I yelled. "Two Grand Slams, Diet Dr. Pepper, and a black coffee with a side of extra bacon. The tip... $1.29. Cheapskate!"

"Ben," she said, a tear going down her cheek.

"Living large, aren't you, Jeanie?"

As I reached toward her, she cowered.

"Go ahead, shove another Grand Slam down your throat, Momma. Huh? Huh?" I said, pounding my fist on the plate as it cracked.

I'd made a scene. The manager was on the phone, glaring at me.

I stood up and approached him. "Do you have something to say?"

“I think someone missed their Xanax,” he said, avoiding eye contact.

“You’ll be missing more than that when I’m through!” I yelled, my heart pounding.

Jean walked out, pacing quickly to her station wagon. I walked back toward the table, dropped an extra five-dollar bill, and grabbed the last bacon strip. I left the car, taking a roundabout path to West Side several minutes later.

# COUCH SURFING

I'd gone to the bar, slung back a few drinks with Ricky that night and we parted ways, trashing Jean and anyone else that crossed our paths at the wrong time. There wasn't any logical point to going home. Hannah would just lecture me on being out too late. So, it was over to Hal's for the night. I'd been dropping in more frequently.

The couch was the place he preferred to sleep most of the time, but he'd slip off to the bedroom when I showed up. I respected the man a great deal. He was all we had left in Hannah's family tree. Somewhere in my drunken musings, I saw some sort of irony that despite our efforts to break the cycle of an only child begetting another only child, we still lost Jake.

I arrived a little after 2 AM. It surprised me to see Hal was still up with a repeat of one of the late-night talk shows playing. We hadn't shared a lot of words—not man to man, one on one. So, nights like this led to different kinds of chats. The dynamics were different. I only confided that the slopes were slippery in my life and time to clear my head was the best medicine.

Hal's abode was cozy. He never set the thermostat below 80 in the summer or above 60 in the winter. That was just the guy he was. I don't think he'd cooked a meal at home since he lost Patricia. That didn't bother him. It enabled him to get out and mingle, to meet people and connect, and rather than wither away and decay like many in his position would, he opted to continue to see and do, and for this, Hannah and I were grateful.

He went on to bed, handing the remote control to me. I turned the TV off. My mind wandered and roamed. There were moments in these hours I swore myself insane and others where I thought I had the greatest epiphanies known to mankind, but I'd be remiss if I didn't admit the voice of Jean, laughing with Hannah and haunting me again and again. My liver screamed for a drink as if hexed. I didn't give in, though.

I needed a glass of water. I was in the midst of a night sweat, probably stress-induced, trying to figure out where to go with the situation with Hannah and Jean. I clicked a lamp on and got up. Everything in the kitchen looked unused for years, only dust bunnies loitering. Hal had a plate, a cup, and a bowl he used perpetually. They stayed in the sink. The rest were just for decoration. I noticed something on his countertop, a paperclip holding some torn-out composition notebook pages together, a flowing cursive leaving me curious.

*I never thought a word like homewrecker could enter my vocabulary. But when you're threadbare on the brink of breakdown, you need something to cope with the stress. For some, it's drugs, for others, alcohol, sex... for me, it's people.*

*Yeah, I know this is going to sound different. Inserting myself into people's lives and doing things to break up the perfect in hopes of making them imperfect. It sounds like something you think couldn't be real, but there are plenty of people like me that need serious help. I mean, I don't have to ramble. We've all hit rock bottom, but how we handle it, that's where it gets interesting. Or, at least, has the potential. Some stories are simpler than others, most stories more forgettable than anything of meaning. And then, there are stories like mine, gobbled up today and digested tomorrow. As you try to purge it from your memory, you're just left with a pit of remorse to follow and wondering why you let me steal your attention away as long as I did.*

*I usually blame my ex, Ricky, but that's not entirely fair because I ruined it, too, convincing myself the only way to make something from nothing was to manufacture it and see if my little weasel would cave. He had the self-control, but I paid extra to make her persistent. I fed her all the information she needed to satisfy, to get him out of my life. Ricky was a simple man that led a simple life — a steadfast laborer. A person with little intent to deviate from the uninteresting. I longed for him to make more of our life together, and he never did. I wanted a pilgrim, a wilderness wanderer. I thought of our years down the road. How many times could we watch the same reruns and movies, and fight about folding towels? He had his way, and I had mine, and honestly, maybe it didn't matter. It shouldn't have. What a dull, pathetic existence. I couldn't stand the thought of being married to the plain vanilla forever. I needed an out. I needed a story, a reason to claim victimhood. Without me, though, he never would have gone off script. He'd be lying in bed snoring in his typical nightly rhythm right next to me while I struggle to get myself comfortable and fight the temptation to smother him. His Fisherman Weekly draped across his face to block my reading lamp. His dirty socks on the floor collecting dust until the next morning just like always. I gripe. He makes an excuse. We both forget and move on, over and over.*

*As for changing things up after we lost our son, Johnny, it remained amicable. We could have lived a million years together and done the same thing every night, and the worst part, he'd still be satisfied. There's something about that that just bothers me.*

*I don't know what made me think he was the right choice. We met in the Dairy Queen lobby. The goof was in a terrible-fitting wash of jeans straight from the Wal-Mart, and enough gel in his slick, thinning hair to make you think it rained all day, every day. The cheapskate was rifling through the newspaper bin. He didn't want to pay. He just wanted to peek at it for free, never picking it up from the rack, just kind of lifting it with a finger and squinting down at it and hoping no one would hold him accountable or make him drop the two quarters our community paper "greedily demanded," as he so eloquently put it — and that annoyed me. I saw him hand the restaurant worker the coupon off the sack for a free ice cream, and that took me to a new level of curiosity and frustration at the same time. I don't discriminate against frugality, but there are certain things that wear me down. It's just the way he was about everything. I think it's because the sack has a little disclaimer on it that says, "cannot be used on current visit," and somehow, he tricks his way into a free cone every time, all on the same visit, mind you. I'd met my opposite. His differing approach to life kept me guessing. Maybe I had it all wrong. It didn't take me long to realize the differing approaches were inferiorities.*

*What motivated me to give him the light of day? Was he mysterious or alluring? Never. He was consistent, though. Maybe it was stability. He was reliable and dependable. A man that needed love and validation. And I gave it to him, sometimes. Until I couldn't bear the simplicity anymore. Give the man a remote control, a TV dinner, and a recliner, and he's set for life. What's he need me for? I'm replaceable. And so, to cure my own boredom, I set him up with her... with Jenna. A little obsessive-compulsive nutball that worked in the fabric department at the JC Penney that should have been shuttered years ago after that stupid commercial.*

*I spotted the little bimbo behind the counter and socialized with her one day on my way to work. We had a cup of coffee. One thing led to another, and we were "friends," on my terms and conditions, of course. It was perfect. I almost patted myself on the back for the find. She was single, dense, and cute. Perfect for Ricky, and even more perfect for a ticket to singlehood. Maybe it was pride that wouldn't let me divorce him for no good reason beyond preference or annoyance. There was nothing interesting about it. No story to tell. I could just hear myself shooting the breeze on the horn to one of the old cows at the beauty parlor.*

*"Oh, yeah. Me and Ricky, we just never got along. So, I divorced him and I'm a lot happier now, he-he. I'll see you at my appointment tomorrow, buh-bye."*

*Heaven help me. That's just awful. It sounds cheap. It sounds selfish. Like something you see in paperback on an endcap in the supermarket for the grannies. I have to protect myself from sounding that way. I want to be relevant. If you're not the victim, your story's not that interesting. Right? So that's exactly what I was doing with Jenna. I was reshaping my story with Ricky, just the way it needed to be, so I could become a better poster child — a victim. Yeah. That's what I needed to become. A victim.*

*I didn't tell him about her, or about our... convergence. Eventually, I worked my way into the plan: to get Jenna after him, to get him weak in the knees, and to ruin our marriage, ceremoniously speaking. I don't know whether she felt all that wholesome about it, but she was single and dumb, and I was at a point where that even sounded appealing to me. And if she had the clap, then Ricky would have it, too. And that was a sort of punishment I could hope for, a good everyday reminder.*

*At first, I kept sending him into the store on his own to get new clothes with a specific budget. He would always settle on the same kinds of shirts and pants — choices so uninspiring I could gag myself, but somehow, instead, chose to tolerate watching this scenario play out. It was a stretch to get him into plaid print, let alone paisley. It was always the friggin' polo shirts. Solid colors and perfect attractions for cat fuzz, food stains, and flaky skin from the face and scalp. And he'd just buy them over and over again. There were subtle differences in the colors he chose, but I soon realized most of that was just a side-effect of discoloration from persistent washing or being sunbaked in the display window because no one else in their right mind would buy them.*

*As for our marriage, we were DOA from day one. I wasn't happy. He wasn't pleased. And we sure weren't making it meaningful in any way beneficial to one another. Aside from cohabiting and sharing the cost of the mortgage, we socialized as well as dim-witted kittens that got gassed a notch too low, escaped the pound, and somehow survived, all the while remaining in the mixed company of one another. And that, is no way to live.*

*No. I didn't have some idealized life on the other side of it planned. It was just freedom that appealed to me. And that was the scary part. I shouldn't want that. I shouldn't need it. I should love my man. He's mine. And you know what? Somehow, I did love him. I just lost my way for a while. It's too late now, though. Feelings waver and falter like the seasons, and families get whiplashed and torn apart... just like that. Torn up and taped together like some kid's wadded up homework with the answers wrong and scratched out.*

*My motive? My motive? Is it your place to ask? Everyone's always asking for motivations and what drives people to mania. The truth here, we're all manipulative at our core. We want what we want. Some of us are just more aware and know how to milk it for all its worth. Curing my boredom takes more handiwork than the flick of a remote. A lot of years married and the best we can quibble over is how badly he parks. I mean, get real here. That's it. I don't think that should bother me. Someone once told me playing it safe was the best choice for me and for him. That going for a man like Ricky would be conservative, and that suited me because that was how they saw me. He'd never hit me. He'd never lie. And he'd never leave. Nope. Never would. He'd just keep sticking around, a real proper Southern gentleman.*

*I had a few coffees with the dummy in the fabric department and had her wrapped around my finger just enough to get what I wanted. She always asked me what I hoped to gain from her relationship with Ricky. I couldn't tell her my reasons. They were too simple. And she was, too. And cheap. I paid the broad two-grand and a couple of cinnamon dolce lattes and there was my ticket to divorce court.*

*You must have some nerve, Jean, I'm sure you're thinking by now. Well, thanks for the observation, I tell myself the same thing. I sure do.*

*It wasn't worth the effort or wasting her limited brainpower to give her a long-winded explanation. She was desperate and so was I. And that commonality would deliver the perfect recipe for a good old-fashioned romance with a hint of steam. And by saying there's a hint of steam coming from Ricky is an overstatement. I mean, I've about convinced myself the man has no creative bones in his body, certainly not behind closed doors. The hemisphere of the brain where that should be firing must have gone to sleep thirty years ago in some critical thinking class. Or maybe it was just a bad bender in the 90s.*

*Getting on with it. They la-di-da'ed one another. He had the ooh's. She had the ah's, and they traded places. The same routine, night after night, for a few weeks. And then I confronted him, because as fate would have it, he came home with the clap. The rat bastard! He never even tried to hide it or lie, never fought for me. And that's when it started to hurt, to break me up inside. That moment I realized my sick, twisted game had reared its ugly head, and I had to face the music.*

*As for them, Jenna played along, all the way down the aisle with Ricky. And they even invited me! Wasn't that sweet? And now, nine months later, he's happily married to the dumb redhead across town in a dilapidated singlewide watching the same damn television shows we used to, spilling beer in her bed instead of mine. And you know what? I'm still grumpy, ugly, and miserable, just like before, ready for a new project.*

*I need that spark again. That rush. My mind drifts to the divorce attorney. Our sad state of affairs. I mean, he's got dozens of these cases, one after the next. A face without color, a voice without sympathy, a heart without feeling, and the deal is done. All because of an impulsive effort to change things up a little.*

*I think back to our day in court. Ricky and I hugged and waved goodbye. There was not much to divvy up. It was cut and dry. Johnny was dead, and we split the piddly life insurance policy right down the middle. We were both employed, and he never disputed the house or the car we owned together. He just up and vanished when I asked. On paper, we were done, dusted, and stored in the district clerk's office with a thousand others side by side in a manila folder with the brads — the same boring vernacular as all the rest. You don't get any of these details, whether juicy or stale. The state doesn't give a damn. Just pay us your fee and get on with it. We don't care. Irreconcilable differences by way of extramarital actions.*

*The judge closed the case. We split... amicably, and I had a story to tell anytime someone asked. There was so little substance to it, though. It was as humdrum as Ricky was. What a mess. That's me, an ugly mess. If you're still interested in talking after all this transparent and brutal honesty, give me a ring. I might be just your kind of thing.*

*Xoxo,*

*Jean*

# DELICATE TOUCH

In a world of coincidences, the letter seemed farfetched. I was just a tool living in some lunatic's larger-than-life delusion. What were the odds a note from Jean would be in my father-in-law's home? Much less a damning one. It felt like a setup. I was too close to crazy to just accept that. Maybe this note was the very thing I could use to show Hannah what Jean was truly capable of. It was validation that somewhere upstairs, a screw was loose. Looser than any of mine. I willfully admit I was due for some maintenance. I didn't know whether I should be bothered that Jean was in touch with Hal, or, thankful. It seemed a sort of divine intervention. What God had brought together, let no one separate, you know, that kind of thing. I suppose it all goes back to point of view and parties willing to accept truths and so on. I planned to broach the subject lightly.

I sat on the couch, looking the note over and over, hearing Jean's voice, thinking of my meeting with Ricky. Hal hadn't mentioned Jean, nor Jean, Hal.

I just didn't know, considering everything, if there was an ideal time to bring it up with him. I decided on the passive approach, laying the note in his reclining chair. I was inches away from photographing it and sending it to Hannah but felt it too much to digest in that format. It would be more appropriate if she heard it straight from Hal or if she had more context.

***

Hal dragged into the room about 8AM somewhat rested while I sat just across on no sleep, pining and wandering the recesses of my mind as the topic of Jean remained untouched. He mumbled something and waved and made a beeline to the coffeemaker. It hadn't been washed in years, not with a scrub brush. Probably not even rinsed. You could see the tan lines on the sides of the pot. He mumbled a minute and groveled out something, but I didn't understand a word of it.

"Coffee?" he said, articulating.

I was a little turned off by the coffee pot, but I knew I'd alienate my host if I dodged it.

I wonder about when people turn down a cup of coffee at someone else's house. Maybe they're not averse to caffeine but just afraid of what else is floating around in it, acknowledging the potential it could be years away from a thorough clean. What is clean, anyway? I guess it's all relative, in the eye of the beholder. Thank God for Hannah. Without her, I can guarantee you wouldn't want anything from mine.

Hal handed me a coffee mug, less washed than the pot. We waited for it to brew. He trotted across the room and sat down in his recliner, fumbling for the remote. Either he was so out of it, he didn't notice, or he was just avoiding it.

"Sleep alright?" he asked.

"No. Not really."

"Oh, yeah? Why's that?"

"Nerves. Just a lot on my mind."

"Well, you know I'm not much for this kind of talk," he said, changing channels on the TV. I think he landed on *Gunsmoke* five seconds before he flipped to *Roseanne*. I studied him for a minute. As the coffee began its percolation cycle, he sighed and looked over at me.

"But, I'm willing to hear you out. You've earned it by taking care of my girl all these years."

He got up, walking back over toward the coffee pot. "Just a bit longer."

"Yeah, thanks, Hal.

He poured some into my mug and then his. "Black is okay with you?"

"Always," I replied.

He came back over to the chair.

"Hey. What's this doing out?" he asked, pulling the partially crumpled letter from Jean from his chair.

"I wanted to talk to you about it," I said. "But I didn't know where to start."

"Why? What's it to you? You read it?"

"Yeah."

"And?"

"Seemed like a depraved mind to me."

"Maybe so," he said, sipping his Colombian roast. "Nice and piping hot."

I drank mine. It was sour to my liking, but plenty strong. Whether that was because of the coffee blend or the layers of coffee film decaying inside Hal's coffee pot, it's unclear. "Yeah. Thank you."

"Depraved mind, huh? Tell me why."

"I mean, the way she belittled her husband, set him up to fail."

"It's all about perspective, Ben. It's always perspective."

"You look at it as if he's the victim. She looks at it like she is because he gave in when put to the test."

"I guess."

"No. You really have to pick a side here."

"Why would I?"

"Because if I'm gonna give you free advice, I need to know you're still treating my daughter well."

"What? Of course I am."

He shook his head at me. "No. No. I see it in your eyes, Ben."

"What are you trying to say?" I asked.

"You need to keep your perspective in check."

"I try. It's an everyday choice."

"Okay. I'll go with that," he said, gulping the rest of his coffee. He stood up and went back to pour another cup. "Top you off?" he asked.

"Sure."

He did so, sitting back down and studying the letter again. "Ben, you know, sometimes, you have to assume the best of someone before you jump to conclusions."

I scoffed. "How can I assume the best when they admit to causing their husband to stumble and make light of their intelligence?"

"We're talking man to man?"

"Yes... And?"

"We have to lead. I'll get burned at the stake for saying this, but who gave the fruit to who, Adam or Eve?"

"What?"

"In the garden."

"I see what you're saying, I guess. Ricky still had to act on it."

"Yep," he said.

"But the whole point wasn't to trip up Ricky, it was to figure out if there was anyone else. Unfortunate to Jean's situation, the guy must have had silly putty for brains and got sucked in."

"Jean's my neighbor. How do you know her?" I asked.

"I don't. I got home from watching Davey one night and found that note jammed between my car seat and the center console."

"Really?"

"Yeah.

"And she just wrote all that to you, a complete stranger?"

"Well, I'm not the worst looking guy, am I? Maybe she spotted me through the window and wanted to tell me I was noticed."

I nodded. "Well, avoid her at all costs. She's not worth it."

"Don't worry about that. Ben, I love my daughter. I know you do, too. And sometimes, people enter our lives that require a different attention and touch. And we don't always know what to do."

"What are you saying?"

"Losing a kid... that's hard, and honestly, I haven't known what to say to you or Hannah. You get my age, and someone's got to lose a spouse eventually, but losing your kid, that's something else entirely. It's enough to drive anyone out of their gourd. I get it."

I nodded.

He topped off my coffee again.

"Hal, I just don't understand it."

"I don't know that we're meant to. It shouldn't happen."

"Well, can you tell Hannah for me?

"Tell her what?"

"Tell her that Jean's a risk to all of us. I mean, this letter, it's a damning confession."

Hal nodded. "I suppose, but that's your soap opera, not mine."

"Hal, the things this woman's done to ruin me. I don't even know where to start."

He sighed. "I'm just not gonna do that. I swore up and down I'd never get in the middle of your drama. Hannah's still my daughter. You've got to do what's best for you and your family — for their safety and security. I can only give advice. I don't have all the answers."

"Do you know what Jean's done already?"

"I don't want to know. Have you gone to the police?"

I scoffed. I was ready to storm out. "No. There are feelings and relationships involved here, and we're in proximity... That gets complicated fast."

"Putting it off, just like everything else."

"What's that supposed to mean?"

"Life gets complicated. People slip up, but I believe there's redemption for those that own their mistakes. And people fall hard in tragedy. It's gonna take some kind of delicate touch to keep the peace around there, considering all I'm hearing."

"Can you help me?" I asked.

"I've done all I can."

"You don't want to rock the boat, do you? Come on, man!" I said, my voice escalating.

"The curtain's already closed on *my* soap opera."

"What?"

"A little before Patricia died, I cheated. She called Hannah, and Hannah just went ballistic, told her she didn't want to know about our problems. That broke her up inside."

"Hal, I'm sorry, I didn't know. She never told me."

"So, all I'm saying is, my character vouching skills mean next to nil."

I shook my head. "I... I'm sorry."

"We've all got our secrets, Ben. Every last one of us. You get me?"

I stood up and set the coffee on the table. "Where do I start?"

"Taller fences make for the best neighbors."

# FENCED IN

On the way out that day, I detoured, taking Hal's advice quite literally. I went down the block to the hardware store and scheduled an appointment for a fence install. We're not talking about a little rinky-dink touch up. I mean, we're talking border patrol caliber stuff here. I found a twelve-foot interlocking board on board fence system. Horizontal rails, bottom rail pickets, posts, and caps all in powder-coated, black, galvanized steel.

No rotting!

No warping!

No splintering!

None of that crap.

It was easier to ask forgiveness later than talk it out and rationalize. I was in the doghouse, anyway. The guy at the store asked for a face-to-face consult to measure it, but I gave him rough estimations and had him order extra just in case. We'd get the fence put in tomorrow and run it all the way up to the street. The picket fence would go away. Screw the local regulations. This was my property. I'd do it my way. Even with both homes on blocks and off the ground three feet, there'd be no more Peeping Thomasina. And we wouldn't have to see her either. No more run-ins watering the grass, weeding the flowerbeds, traipsing out to get the newspaper, or watching stupid Gonzo do his business in the yard. So liberating. You didn't ask for much in these situations. You just wanted to have that moment to yourself without exploding into a rage over something trivial and of literally no consequence to you. The fence might not stop the coffee chats or the occasional drop-ins, but it would squash the casual violations of privacy. And it would send a message. That's for damn sure.

"We won't be your perfect little family anymore, will we?" I mumbled, looking over the order invoice. "It was good until you came in and ruined it. You wrecked it... turned us into your little devil's playground. I can't take that anymore..."

I channeled Jerry Blake from *The Stepfather*. "All we need is a little order around here..."

***

I fell asleep in my study, knowing I was better off undiscovered when the workers showed up to put the new fence in. It would peeve half the block, but I didn't care, and neither did the contractor I hired. He must have been desperate for cash or ripping me off, one of the two. Either way, I just wanted it done. To get the eyesore of a house out of my peripheral, and my family's personal life off Jean's radar. I heard the truck pull in early that morning. I knew the earful was coming. A new fence wouldn't be the issue, but the chosen color, texture, and height of said fence would. So, I guess this forever ends the most important element of the debate between men and women. Size matters... but too much is too much.

I took the day off from work, not for the scourging but to enjoy the satisfaction of the progress. I peered through the window off and on, watching the workers as they pieced it together seamlessly. The supervisor I'd met at the hardware store did a lot more standing around and barking orders than he did working. I kept wondering if Jean would come over, but I guess she was out that morning and it was to our collective benefit because there would be little time for a confrontation during the install. By lunch hour, the new fence was up, the contractor handed me the invoice, and his workers were tossing remnants of our white pickets into the back of their truck carelessly.

I handed him a check. "Some of those might have been salvageable."

"Yeah. I know," he said, "but my cousin, I call him Lurch, he's not right in the head anymore. Just a hired hand, so you know, it is what it is. I get to watch while he sweats, and I still make more an hour than he does."

"How kind of you," I muttered.

"No, man, it's not like that. My back, it's killing me all the time." The contractor pulled out a cigarette and lit it. "So, what's the deal, man?"

"With what? I paid you."

"No. Don't get me wrong, but I mean, you must be really bothered by your neighbor to put up a fence that high in a residential area like this. I think the city height limit is ten feet, but we'll just say I got lazy with measurements and my name is Lurch, and I'm some drifter passing through town. And if we ever see each other again or if you want to hire me again, I'll be Herman and then... Dale Cooper. You catch my drift? I know you probably got other odd jobs around here."

"I got something even better," I said, pulling out a pack of Garashock 500s.

"Are you seriously trying to bribe your contractor with painkillers?"

"No. I'm trying to sell my contractor painkillers. It's my job. I cure all the pain with my little blue pill."

"That's a different little blue pill, my man. Ha-ha!" he said.

"Garashock is the future. If you've got any bank accounts in this country, you'd suit yourself to invest."

"What are you trying to say, man? That I don't operate a legit business?"

"Nah... just that there are opportunities to grow your income if you play the markets."

"I don't do that high finance shit. I'm self-made."

"I can respect that."

"All done," the affectionately deemed Lurch called out in a tone of voice comparable to his namesake.

"Goodbye, little blue pill man. Hope you can still get it up like your fence without it. Ha-ha!"

"I'll do my best. Still in the doghouse... won't be out anytime soon."

"Been there, buddy. Hang in there and enjoy your new fence!"

I zoned out.

I'd taken Jake to the movies — our first bloody action flick together. I'd told Hannah it was PG-13 fare, but it was actually an anniversary showing of *Rambo* in all of its macho glory. I never saw my boy flinch or cringe. He took it like the man he'd become. On the ride home that night we got our stories straight so Hannah would be convinced we'd gone to see another sports flick showing that she'd have little interest in.

“I’m proud of you, Son. You’ll make a great father one day,” I said, patting him on the shoulder as we drove home.

***

There was no ideal time to go inside. I’d waited a few hours after the fence was installed for the shock to wear off. I came in and sat down. I looked at Hannah.

She was looking closely at something.

“Dad mailed this. It arrived earlier,” she said. She handed me the envelope. It was Jean’s note. In the upper margin, he’d handwritten his own comment on a sticky note clasped on top.

*Hannah,*

*I know it means next to nothing coming from me... but I figured you ought to take a look, all things considered.*

*Love,*

*Dad*

I hugged her. We walked over to the couch and sat down. I took her hand.

She sighed. “I’ve just been embarrassed. I didn’t know where to start, Ben. I kept thinking about your track history. How the behaviors and patterns didn’t match up, but some selfish part of me wanted to see myself as the victim. You, the perpetrator. Kind of like the letter.”

“It’s all about mindset,” I said. “We’re all victims if we want to be. And the reality of the matter, we *can* choose not to be. Circumstances come and go, it’s mostly science at work. The art is being able to tell the difference between what’s manufactured and what’s genuine.”

“So, what are we dealing with here? Art or science?”

“I don’t know,” I said. “I guess it’s a bit of both.”

“I got to thinking about it. That day we were looking at yearbooks. Jean kept laughing and commenting about how much you’d changed and telling me how much I hadn’t.”

“It doesn’t take a rocket scientist to play the devil’s matchmaker,” I said.

“Why go to such lengths?”

"Desperation to disrupt."

"But why us?" she asked.

"We lost our son and we're together. She lost her kid, and she's divorced."

"There's got to be more than that," she said. "You think she did all of this out of envy or spite?"

"No, but Jean Jackson has a day job with the state. These people go postal sometimes."

"So, considering the note, have you talked yet?"

"No. I'm not ready to."

"I noticed the curtains were closed," I said.

"And that honking fence... What the hell is that?"

"Privacy. We need more of it. I just hope it sends a message."

She sighed and rolled her eyes. "It does. I appreciate a man that will protect me and our Davey," she said, looking away.

I didn't know what it was, but she struggled to make much eye contact that night. We all carried our burdens in our own ways, and rather than make her feel like I was observing the pattern, I minimized instead. As we embraced, I felt a tightness in Hannah. I leaned in to kiss her.

I looked to the side for a second and took a deep breath. "Honey, there's one more thing I need to talk to you about."

"What is it?" she asked.

"Mori wants to throw a party here. And I kind of already committed us to doing it."

"Okay. I can get on board with that. It's a beautiful house. We have a great backyard for it."

"Yeah. I kind of... might have scheduled it for tomorrow."

"You what?" she said, picking up one of her throw pillows and tossing it at me.

"Yeah... I'm sorry. I know that was stupid."

She sighed. "Just work people and their families, right? Twenty to twenty-five?"

"Well, it's probably like forty to forty-five. I invited some neighbors, too."

"What... why?"

"I just thought it would be good to mingle with the people that are close by, too. You know, rather than host three or four separate affairs, let them all cross currents. We always try to segregate these types of things, but I think that cripples us from really... cross pollinating."

"Cross pollinating, huh? Are you sure that's the right move?"

I raised my eyebrows and nodded. "Positive."

"Alright, Ben. You've got work to do."

"I'm sorry. I know I should have talked with you first about the party, but I called the meat market and they're holding the barbecue for us. I'll just go down and pick it all up and we'll have a cleaning party tonight."

"*You* will... and maybe Davey, if you bribe him with enough candy," she said. "I'm not the one that set up this oversized event on such short notice, knucklehead, but I'll indulge your request to be present and cute — Maybe even a little peppy if they're lucky and I'll pour on the charm just the way you've always wanted."

"That's fair. One more thing... I didn't invite Jean."

"Well, that's okay with me," she said. "She's going to show up anyway, you know. It'll be too much for her not to."

"Yeah... that's the point.

"Whatever, Ben. I'm taking a few hours for myself tonight to paint. You've got this under control, right?"

# PARTY ON THE PATIO

A row of fourteen cars were parked on either side of our extended driveway next to the new fence. Hannah and I left the back gate open for guests to come and go at their leisure. Mori paid for a bounce house, and I'm certain everyone for five blocks could smell the barbecue. It was a casual affair. I was in blue jeans and a Poison t-shirt. Hannah was dolled up in a summer dress. Davey made sure everyone that came got a tour of the house, the backyard, and my untidy garage. It didn't bother me. It was kind of sweet. Our little host in action, I mean.

There was one thing that made the night even better. Jean wasn't invited, but Jose who lived next to her was, and Tonya, who lived on the opposite side catty-corner to us, was as well, along with her schnauzer pup, Stooge. It wouldn't be a party without Nina, the petite woman that lived behind us and screamed at her dogs every night to shut the blank up. As it turned out, she made a mean Cuban coffee. Jean had been such a time suck; we hadn't gotten to know any of them. They were all "evil," "weirdos," or "creeps". I wondered what *we* were by her definition. She was the source of all wisdom and knowledge — until that night. The party would certainly prove a point. It was unorthodox but just like Mori and I decided, we mixed and matched the company people with neighbors, hoping it would send a message and normalize things. We had most of the usuals from Olkov there, Mori, a little bookworm from accounting named Kerri, and somehow, the shrimp-loving, Bob Dowdy. No, we didn't invite rent-a-cop. I didn't need someone keeping track of how many beers were consumed or if the cigars were legal or not. Natasha was there, too, playing with the kids in the bounce house. Somehow, this all felt like a path to normalcy, like something we could do annually. If Jean decided not to crash the party and would be a part of it on our terms and conditions, I might allow it — if she played her cards right.

I wanted a Caribbean themed playlist, so I found the *Scarface* soundtrack and had it blaring. There were some good numbers on that. Everything came full circle when Nina came up behind me and handed Mori and me a pair of Cuban cigars. We lit up, dancing and smiling in a lighthearted sort of way, in sync with the music.

Hannah and I made eye contact. She moved closer to Mori and the two of them danced hand in hand. She pulled the cigar from his mouth and handed it to me. I laid it down on the edge of the barbecue pit. As for Nina, her friendliness was likely just because I'd sold her a tall bottle of 500s in a pill mill across town at half price.

The song ended and Mori came back over to me and picked up his cigar. "So good," he said, smiling, the cigar between his thumb and index finger. The song changed from a salsa infused tango to another 80s song.

"Ben, we've got problem..."

"What's that?"

"Give me phone. Music is bad."

He cued up a number from my grade school days.

"First album. Backstreet Boys!"

"What? Are you kidding me, Mori?"

"No way! These guys... huge in Europe."

"Like twenty-five years ago, man... Quit playin' games with my heart," I said, sing songy.

Mori laughed and puffed on his cigar. "See, Ben, this is where it's at. This works! Hmm-hmm."

A cluster of buzzed guests huddled around the cooler, talking trash about the basketball game the previous night. Mori and I chimed in, off and on as we could. He slipped across the yard to visit with Bob Dowdy, and I lost track.

The back fence squeaked as it clicked shut. In that moment, it seemed like all eyes gravitated that way. Jean came in, dressed in her every day, All-American girl sort of look, her blue jeans a size too small, her shirt a tad on the snug side.

Hannah walked toward her, acting bouncy and peppy, almost excited to see her. She seemed annoyed with the music in the background but hadn't asked me to turn it down. There was a certain groove most people had on the patio. If you weren't tuned in, you were missing out.

I eavesdropped while I finished the next round of barbecue on the pit.

"Hey, Jean," Hannah said.

"Hey. When were you going to tell me about the... that... fence?"

Hannah shook her head. "It's not my doing. Talk to Ben."

She came over toward me. I expected a confrontation, but it never happened. Perhaps she was just so thrown by the party she couldn't muster it. Or our little altercation at Denny's was still fresh on the mind.

I looked over and waved. "Hey, Jean!"

"I just thought I'd stop by," she said. "I saw the cars pulling in and had to see for myself."

Hannah came and bailed me out. "Yeah. I'm sorry Ben didn't send an invitation. I meant to tell you about this the other day," she lied. "Work function."

"It can't just be work. There are neighbors here. People I warned you about," she said, her teeth gritted.

"Well, we thought we'd give them a shot," I replied. "That's our business."

Jean handed Hannah a sack. "I thought Davey might enjoy this little gift from me and Gonzo. It's his birthday, right?"

"Well, thanks so much," Hannah said. "It's not his birthday, but he loves presents. Why don't you stick around and have some barbecue?"

"I better go," she said, the growing awkwardness in her voice speaking volumes.

"Come on, Jean," Hannah said.

I poured fuel on the fire. "Yeah, Jean. Let's make you a plate. We'll get you some barbecue, beans, potato salad, maybe a cold one? You can take it home if you don't want to stay. We made enough food to feed half the block."

"How kind of you. I try not to drink in public, though."

I smiled. "Alright. I'll whip up a plate and throw in some scraps for Gonzo."

"That's nice. You don't have to. I just wanted to say hi."

She walked over and gave me an awkward side hug, making sure every curve was pressed against me. I hugged her back and gave her shoulder a firm pat.

"Glad you could stop by, Jean," I said.

"Yeah," she said. Her daggers stared me down, but she kept on her best behavior, probably knowing she was on the brink of party-crashing. I shoveled a variety of foods from the buffet onto her plate and handed her a diet soda.

"Why don't you take a seat and hang out a while? You know some of the neighbors, right?"

"I wouldn't want to be a burden."

I shook my head.

"Alright. Sure," she said. She stood there close, like she didn't get the memo that I didn't want her there.

"What did you think about the game last night?" she asked, forcing conversation as I rotated the pork ribs on the grill. I basted them with a sauce that brought the flavor full circle.

"It was close," I said. "I prefer *Hoosiers*. You follow sports that close?"

"Yeah. I'm a hometown girl. I love to cheer on the regional favorites."

"It's been sloppy lately, though. May be about time for a change at the top of the house. Coach running his mouth too much about politics and not focused on the game anymore."

"Yeah, the front office is always fluid," she replied, clearly using bigger words to sound smarter.

"Try one of these ribs. Careful, they're still hot," I said, handing one over to her.

The unease I saw in her eyes dissipated when I got her on sports.

Mori disengaged, excusing himself out the back gate earlier than I expected. He kissed Hannah on the cheek and left without a goodbye. Natasha followed, waving briefly.

Jean bit a piece of the rib and grabbed a wet napkin from the table behind me. "Oh, Gosh. Benjamin, these are fantastic. Your sauce. Remarkable!"

"It's nothing. Just a weekend habit. Parties are a great chance to show off a little."

"I like when you show off," she said.

I looked away, making myself look busier on the grill than I was. Eventually, she left.

Bob Dowdy migrated toward me, and that's when I realized Jean wasn't the worst conversationalist — in my head or in person.

"Hey there, plug-ola. Great party, my man," he said, his words slurred.

"You know it."

"And your grill's not the only thing sizzling back here. These ladies... mmm!"

"Bob, go bounce some of that alcohol out of you or something," I said.

He laughed, slapping me on the back. The joker got into the bounce house. I never inspected its contents before it was hauled away that night, but I'm sure it wasn't pretty, and Bob looked greener when he came out. I suppose I got some satisfaction from that.

Hannah disappeared. Probably inside in protest because I'd let things run longer than I should, but I still felt like this party was therapy for all of us.

As Davey and I farewelled most of the guests for the last hour, I had this feeling inside I was too hard on Jean. That I'd dehumanized her.

# FAMILY RULES

There was an unspoken rule in my family growing up. "Do whatever you want, when you want, just don't get caught when it ain't right." Like any child, my moral compass often wandered, waxing and waning with the seasons. No sense of purpose or direction offered me by my mother or my father — nothing beyond scathing or scolding when something inside snapped at the wrong moment. I was different, though. I could break the vicious cycle and overcome this generational habit. The overwhelming knot in the pit of my stomach reminding me every day I still had a conscience, a way to overcome it all, running from the deception, the drama, and the evil. And every time I resisted, a monster within still lingered, waiting for the right moment to devour the goodwill I kept stored away.

After Davey was tucked in for the night, I wrapped up cleaning the back porch alone — trashing countless beer bottles, throwaway paper plates, and diet sodas crushed all over the yard.

Jean whispered in my mind.

*Why'd you let me down like that? You know I don't handle that well.*

"I don't know," I muttered. "It was instinct."

I sat down and cracked open a beer — the October heat that night lingering like an overbearing friend that didn't get the cue to leave. Hannah came outside. She said little but opened a beer and sat by me.

"I'd say that went pretty well," I said, looking at her and dropping my hand on top of hers.

"Yeah. I guess so. It's hard to get a good conversation in with so many around," she said.

"It's all about quantity over quality at these kinds of things."

"That goes without saying," she said, taking a larger sip on the booze than I expected.

"You invite one co-worker; you invite all of them. Otherwise, some idiot's feelings get hurt if they find out," I said, chugging the rest of my beer and pitching it in the bulging garbage sack. It's clanking all too familiar.

"Some idiot, huh?"

"Yeah," I said, opening another beer.

"So, do you want to talk about why you didn't invite the 'idiot' living next door to your bizarro 'work meets neighbors' social function you conveniently 'forgot' to tell me about until the last minute?"

"We've seen plenty of her and not enough of the others. Too much of one point of view is dangerous. It's unhealthy. It's good to be around a variety of people. To hear their insights, their flaws. Not a soul on this planet's perfect."

"Gonna turn philosopher on me?" she asked.

"If that's what you need. Did you have a nice time?"

She nodded. "It was good. You're right. I need to spend more time around people. It's good for me, you, and us."

"I'm glad you see it that way. Make sure you try the sample plate, before deciding which dish is your favorite."

"You actually have a few good words tonight, Mr. Decker. I might keep you," she said.

I smiled. "I hope so." I perused the porch, noticing the gift sack from Jean.

Hannah looked that way. "Forgot about Jean's gift, didn't we? Davey's birthday?"

"Well, she was only about eight months off. There's a good friend for you," I said. "I mean, I know we've pulled a random POS off a shelf or two in our time and said it was a gift."

Hannah slapped my hand. "Stop it, Ben," she said, rifling through inordinate amounts of red tissue paper. She pulled out a black spined book with silver emblazoned script lettering.

*The Divine Comedy.*

I reached for it immediately.

"This book for a six-year-old kid?" I asked, leafing through it. "This stuff's a little heady... even for me and you."

"Don't sell me short, Ben Decker," she said, snippily. "I once was a student of literature."

"Weren't we all?"

"Whether we wanted to or not, pretty much," she said, smiling.

As I made eye contact with her, I noticed how much the color to her face seemed flushed, how her eyes drooped, how there was a lot I'd missed in my fixation with Jean. And I was sorry about that.

Thumbing halfway through the book, I spotted a slew of troubling illustrations of the afterlife, portrayed through the eyes of Dante Alighieri.

"Are you okay?" she asked, using the back of her hand to wipe off my accumulation of forehead sweat.

"I think so. This book, it just gives me the creeps," I said, squeezing at the back of my neck.

"Didn't she say that was from her... and Gonzo?" Hannah asked.

"Yeah."

"It seems off-color. A book like this is too much for a kid," she said.

"I've been telling you I've had concerns about her. Are you ready to confront her? I mean, considering everything?" I asked.

She shook her head. "No, Ben, I think it's time you speak up for a change. This is a matter of our child's well-being and I deem that a family security issue. Hence, I defer to you. Oh, Ben, the mighty lord over 1737 17th Street."

"Fine. I'll go over tomorrow and have a chat."

She nodded. "Thank you, Ben."

"Difficult or not. Some conversations need to be had."

# REAL TALK

The next morning, I opted for a remote workday to catch up. I didn't do that often enough. There was a tap on the door to my study. I opened it. There was no one there. Peeking out the window, I noticed the Range Rover still parked in the driveway next to the Mercedes. I stepped onto the back patio. My heart sunk when I saw the stack of papers.

NOTICE OF INTENT TO FILE DIVORCE

*Ben,*

*I'm giving this to you to let you know I'm ready for a divorce. I've put up with things as long as I could, and I can come to no better conclusion. You've misrepresented yourself frequently and recent events have further evidenced your inability to practice self-control with other women. We have two options.*

*Traditional Divorce*

*Part-as-Friends Divorce*

*Review the following pages and determine which will work best for you.*

*I still want you to be a part of Davey's life, but I cannot and will not tolerate any more of your infidelities and indiscretions.*

*Hannah*

I flipped through it briefly. A stack of evidence was piled up and organized neatly. At the top, a black-and-white photograph of me at the West Side motel,

Natasha hunched over the side of the car in a risqué dress, the DateMeHoney profile, all the messages printed and stapled together, stacks of e-mails with Tina, an invoice to the LadyLove subscription, and a picture of Mori and I sitting in a restaurant booth with red x's over our eyes. The check with Hannah's separate account pushed me over the edge. I chunked the packet on the ground. I would fight it with every breath in my body to make sure it wouldn't end without a fight. I was ready to let her have it. Before I could muster words, I heard Jean's voice.

*Oh, Ben. Are you that surprised? You've been putting off the inevitable. It was only a matter of time. You're well paid. You have it all. And now she won't be there to nag, nag, nag. And you and I, we'll have plenty of time to get more acquainted. Your life will be so quiet, you won't know what to do. And that's the perfect time for me to visit. Ha-ha!*

A dryness hit the back of my throat as my heart raced. This wasn't the way it would end. I loved Hannah and Davey. Nothing would drive my family apart if I had anything to do with it. It wasn't Hannah. She wasn't this deluded. She would have talked through this with me first. We would have been adults about it, and considering the letter, I thought I was redeemed.

"You've taken this thing too far, bitch!" I yelled, coming around the new fence and into Jean's yard, firing my gun in the air. The Saturday Night Special would be plenty to take her out. I'd put the bullet right through her stupid head and end her. She'd finally get the devil's due.

I entered 1739. It was darker and much worse than I remembered. I flipped the switch off and on multiple times, but the lights weren't working. A rat ran across the room and then I saw the roaches on the far walls. Maybe Jean just stopped paying the bills, and we hadn't noticed. A sleeping bag was spread across the couch. A long extension cord came through the window from another property down the block on the opposite side of the old television. *Jerry Springer* was on with the volume maxed out. Piles of melted candle wax were all over the floor having dripped and dried in multiple spots. There were rows of candle nubs on the windowsills and all throughout the house. The stubby beer bottles were everywhere. Some tossed against walls. Others broken into pieces. The rest, intact but empty. On the kitchen counter, I spotted a burner phone that looked like the one I'd snapped before. I heard Jean's voice. I think it was through the speakerphone, but it was hard to tell.

*Oh, Benjamin, you knew it had to come to this. Everyone's got to face the music, baby... to get what they've always longed for. It's all about you. It's all for you. It always was, darlin'.*

My gun was ready. Jean came in from the back room, a candle lit in her hand.

"Barge right in, why don't you?" I mumbled.

She leaned over, lighting another before I could get to her.

"Is that the best you're gonna do, Benjamin Decker? Shoot me? Eight hundred seventy-three million ways to kill a woman and you choose a damn gun?"

"It's what you deserve, homewrecker! Choke on this!"

Aiming at her head, I pulled the trigger. Jean just stood there. She never flinched, and neither did I.

There was no entry point in the skull.

No exit wound.

No pool of blood.

And no satisfaction.

There was also no way I missed. The hole in the wall behind her confirmed that. My gun was working just fine.

Gonzo barked loudly in the back room. I lunged toward Jean and the candles dropped to the floor, catching the curtain on fire behind us. We were struggling — tossing and tumbling on the floor, grunting, hemming, and hawing like animals romping in the hay after dark. Jean was stronger and heftier than I could have guessed, as she wrapped her arms around me and screamed. We huffed and puffed as even our sweat gasped for air and the flames choked us out.

Hannah screamed from outside the window. "Ben! Stop!"

Jean Jackson, the woman in 1739, had ruined us.

Hannah plowed in through the front door, her phone ringing through to 911 as I panted heavily, and Jean laid on the floor, winded.

"I'm not gonna let you ruin my family," Hannah yelled.

I pointed the gun at my head. "I'm not gonna let *me* ruin my family... not anymore."

"Ben, please! Don't do this. It doesn't have to be this way!" Jean yelled, tears streaming down her cheeks. She ran toward me, grabbing at the gun as my finger found the trigger again.

“I’m ready to see Jake,” I called out as my eyes met with Hannah’s. “I love you.”

Hannah moved through the flames in a rush toward us.

“Stop!” she yelled.

I pulled the trigger, collapsing to the ground.

I always imagined I’d hear the click and just before impact, that louder pop as I crossed over. The click was all it took. Jean vanished away.

My worlds converged in a whirlwind.

I sat in 1739 alone late one night, drunk, popping little blue pills and writing a letter, concocting a memory of Jean and Ricky, a man I’d met in support group, and the red-headed bimbo from Sacramento, the whole affair a way to rationalize a parallel self-sabotage. He never met me in the bar. It was just me and the 500s. I left the note in Hal’s car in hopes it would jar him to come back to Hannah and mend her cracks.

It all faded to black.

# FLICKER AND FLASH

Riding in the ambulance, my memories were thrown.

"Just another fever dream," I said, popping the blue pill.

The television in 1739 blared, the darkening curtains blocking all visibility from the outside. *Jerry Springer* ran on repeat, the show's reported calamities supercharging the fuel for my madness.

Hovering under the candlelight, I wrote feverishly in a one-hundred-page composition notebook.

Jean yelled. *You've got to give me more. I need more. It's too soft, Benjamin. You're too soft, Benjamin. I guess Daddy's hand was never heavy enough. Was it?*

Sometimes I'd get worked up and scream. "I'm trying. I'm trying. I've almost got this," I'd reassure. "You're the one hampering things. I can't hit my groove with you bogging me down."

*Ah-Ah*, she said.

I jotted another note in Miss Jean's cursive handwriting.

*CONFRONT WITH PHOTOGRAPH,*
*STAGE SCENE WITH NATASHA, WEST SIDE*

I tore out the page and folded it.

I'd sketched the following week's plot. It just made it easier for us that way. "Real Jean" was burning the midnight oil at both ends, the unappreciated and underpaid government worker she was. Though I wanted to give her what she needed to flourish, the minutia wore me down, and I faded as quickly as I arrived.

I took the sheet to Denny's. The corner booth had always been the drop-off point, jammed between the wall under the window in the southwest corner. We never visited there, though, not until the confrontation, at least. I left the first note on a whim.

*Are you looking for a new sort of spark? A big change in your life? I'm a burned out worker at company X. I'm looking for another burned out worker at company Y to do something unconventional with. Please note, it will require a full performance in a suburban residential setting. If this sounds crazy, call me. If it doesn't, don't bother, and miss the adventure. I'll pay well. Remember, no matter how hard it gets, the better you do, the more we accomplish. This'll bring that spark back; I promise you that!*

*Call or Text, 478-6123*

The note sat there for two weeks before I got the call. I guess that's when Jean found it. Thus comes the story where two corporate drones of the opposite sex eat in the same chain diner at different hours, their blank expressions not so dissimilar, their jobs killing them slowly, and the desire to break monotony comes to fruition. We sought another way to cure the inevitable path to madness, and I suppose that's where the trouble really was. I had the money; she had the time, and together, we brought the story to life.

Just as the great light in the sky beckoned, I came back to my senses, my heart pounding rapidly, my vision blurred. Hannah came into focus just above.

"Thank God I didn't buy American," I said, weakly.

# RESTLESS LEG SYNDROME

After a few hours in the hospital, Hannah and I had just arrived home. She seemed distant. Maybe it was just trauma, some kind of aftershock from all the things we'd been through.

"They said the smoke inhalation should clear up by the end of the week," I said, my voice scratchy and worn.

"Good," she said, pulling out her keys and unlocking the house. "I dropped Davey with dad... We finally talked. We really talked."

"Yeah?"

"Yeah. It was good to catch up. Mom kept him so pinned-up all those years, I felt like I was meeting a new man."

"I'm glad to hear that. He loves you, Hannah."

She nodded. "I love him."

"Good."

We were still in some kind of limbo; I knew that.

We finished our evening routine and prepped to rest for the night. I flipped channels on the television, needing diversion from the recent stressors. Hannah and I hadn't exchanged words in over an hour.

She finally broke the silence. "Things got weird for a while, didn't they?"

"With your dad?"

"No. With us, Ben. Where's your head?"

"Everywhere and anywhere all at once," I said. "An ugly blue haze."

"I know," she said, looking away a second. "You weren't great at pulling the pill packets from your pockets."

"Why didn't you say something?"

"They mellowed you out, and a less neurotic Ben is a better Ben."

"What?"

"We need to talk," she said, her eyes glued on the ceiling fan as it spun in unrelenting circles. "I don't know where to start."

"The truth?"

A tear went down her cheek. "That night we lost Jake. The little blue pills in your aspirin bottle... I knew they weren't aspirin. And you probably thought I gave one to Jake that night, but I didn't."

I struggled to process the statement. "You what?"

"I said I didn't give Jake the pills from your aspirin bottle. I knew they were the 500s. Honestly, I was so stressed out and put out with your indifference, I took one, then two, and then a few hours after that, three. That's when I saw him. My mind wandered and turned, took me to hell, spun me up in all kinds of circles. There was something about that night, Ben... Something that told me it was over before it happened — that he was gone. And I never knew what to say, or how to admit it. To admit that I failed him... That I failed you... and that I failed Davey. I've been lifting samples from your car for months. Those big boxes in the trunk. I know you think you're in tune with everything, some kind of stellar observer, but you've been a thirty-thousand-foot guy a long time. You never keep a perfect inventory. You fly by the seat of your pants, and I've taken advantage. I've been in my own ugly blue haze. Saying things I shouldn't. Doing things I shouldn't. Hating people I shouldn't. It just... cured my insanity, Ben. It made my paintings come to life. I haven't even showed you half of them. Socializing with Jean felt like 3D. And the coffee, it just made the coffee taste so much better."

A tear went down my cheek. "I... I don't know what to say. I'm sorry for not noticing the right things, for getting wrapped up in everything else. It's so easy to get selfish and hyper focus. I got loaded that day, too. I felt so off-kilter. I swore I'd never do it again, but I tricked myself into thinking I wasn't. It just felt like a dream. Those samples beckoning in the darkest hours of the night... me giving in when I couldn't sleep."

"Don't redirect my mistakes," she said. "I screwed up. I owe you a lot for helping me navigate this mess, for speaking with dad when I wouldn't, and for sticking by my side. I'm sorry for believing at any point that the nutjob next door was my friend. I guess it was just the pills talking."

I nodded. "She wasn't a nutjob."

"What's that?" she asked.

"Jean's not a nutjob."

"What?"

"Yeah, uh, Jean was just a woman I hired."

"No!" she said, grabbing my arm. "You're kidding."

Hannah ran her fingers through her hair, taking a deep breath.

"I own 1739. I bought it a few months before we moved in here. I wanted to hire some contractors to fix it up and flip it."

"And you never told me?"

"I'm sorry. I know I should have."

"I've got another question, though. What were you doing in there? The gun... the yelling... the tumbling. Jean wasn't even home..."

"It's hard to blame nature. It's hard to blame nurture, but you can always blame your neighbor."

"Huh?"

"I never measured up, Hannah. You've always stooped down. I'm a self-aware slacker. And I guess, somewhere in my cracked subconscious, I thought freeing you from the burden of me would help you grieve and heal the way you needed to. There was just some part of me too deluded to admit it. I know it was stupid. The pills. They've muddied my thoughts, my judgment, my center of gravity, and my presence. *That's* addiction."

Hannah shook her head. "Ben, I did enough wrongs of my own. Can we just start with a clean slate?"

"I'll do your crazy, if you'll do mine," I said, smiling.

We embraced.

# NEW BEGINNINGS

After the incident I deemed "The Great Fire of 1739," I quit my job with Olkov and got into real estate full time. I'd sell a new pleasure that would be less addicting and offer people a more fulfilling happiness than a little blue pill ever could.

I was around the house, less buried in work, and a lot more engaged in everyday life. Jake would have wanted that. Davey appreciated it, too. I made most of his soccer games, packed his lunches in the mornings, and even took care of dishes and laundry. We were still on a first name basis with our takeout drivers but made efforts to cook a meal together as a family at least twice a month.

Hannah sold lots of colorful paintings from her 1739 series. We stayed in 1737. I over-watered my perfect St. Augustine Grass. I even fought the city three times to let me keep the fence. Joe Levens, my professional ambulance chaser, took us across the finish line. Neither of us donned a blue jacket special in court, either.

As for 1739, it sat vacant again and was fire damaged, but remained salvageable. I gave Real Jean the Dopey Hummel as a peace offering, which fetched $5,000 from an antique dealer. She still doesn't want much to do with me.

At some point, I realized it was time to evaluate friends and enemies the same way I'd lectured my sons. The best and worst often hover close and it's a challenge to distinguish the two. The guy that has nothing to do with you or sits on a different wavelength, avoiding you entirely might not actually be your enemy at all, but a caring citizen giving you the courtesy of not bogging you down with his differences. You never have to know. It's insignificant.

There was no ugly shootout when I left Olkov, nor a confrontation. Apparently, I'd gotten that out of my system at a Denny's on the west side of town more than once. My exit was quiet, a diplomatic resignation, a friendly farewell, and a damn good off the books cash severance. I let sleeping dogs lie when I walked out, and I'm glad I did.

Within a couple of months, Mori ended up in federal prison along with Natasha, Bob Dowdy, and the greater majority of Olkov Enterprises, our little blue pill crumbling away. Everyone, except the dad gum rent-a-cop, who somehow kept a job with the next company that arrived. Ben-Buster returned to 1737, inventoried, itemized, and organized in all of its glory. Less the cracked copy of *Mystery Men.* I charged Bob Dowdy a fee for that before they locked him up.

For a short period, I functioned under the belief that I, too, would find my way into Olkov's messy indictments, but somehow Mori had me listed as a third-party contractor. I guess he always liked me the most. Sometimes, you just end up lucky. I answered a few minor questions outside of court and that was the end of it. Even in prison, Mori's likability remained at least 4.6% because of his selling the warden on premium bedsheets for the entire joint. And that alone took him 2.2% higher amongst the prisoners and a solid 18% more than Bob Dowdy, who maintains a negative number to this day.

I was preparing to show another house across town one morning when I saw Ricky arrive at 1739. I waved and stepped out of the car. He approached. After he looked me over a few times, he came closer to shake hands.

"Realtor, huh?" he said. "Why not just say you're the guy next door? I would've told you the same thing either way."

"I am a realtor now," I said. "But you're right, I'm sorry. Where's Jean?"

"She lived here her whole life. And I mean every single day," he said. "I hope to God she did find someplace else. Old properties, family history, all that stuff... it gets complicated quick, man. She wrote me a letter. It came in last night. I guess this is as much as we'll ever know."

*Ricky, oh, My Richard,*

*I failed you. And I know this now. Montana's nice this time of year, and that's where Gonzo and I drop our plows.*

*With complicated love,*

*Jean.*

*P.S. - Tell the bimbo from Sacramento that I appreciate her. That I liked the Cinnamon Dolce Lattes. And that even though she ruined us, that was my own doing. There are some paisley printed ties in the dresser inside, and I expect you to wear them. My new journey starts now. Keep the house and fix it up. And wish Ben, Hannah, and Davey the best of luck.*

I didn't want to tell him. I wasn't ready.

"Hmm," I said, handing it back. "Well, what are you thinking about all this?"

"I don't know yet," he said. "I'm sure not gonna chase after that loon. We'll keep the house, though."

"Alright, neighbor, until next time, then."

I waved at him and turned around. Hannah was on the porch chatting with another red-headed woman about ten years her senior. She was cute but over-caffeinated and talking six hundred thirty-seven words a minute.

"Yeah, and that's when I told my Ricky that we'd ditch the old trailer across town and move in over here. I'll get the prettiest curtains, and we'll paint the walls the most wonderful pastels, and be the best neighbors anyone could ever ask for. I can bring you coffee, make you dinner, and get you discounts at the store, too. Whatever you need!"

I ran my fingers across the top of my head and looked over at Hannah again. The red-headed woman wasn't there.

"Who were you talking to?" she asked.

"No one," I replied, taking a deep breath.

I smiled. Her grin told me all I needed to know.

A little imagination never hurts anyone. Broken people are beautiful, too.

# LINGERING TERRORS

There are nights I struggle, and a little blue pill wants to own me. Unhealthy thoughts harassing me in my darkest hours. Times that I want to find resolve on a given day, and it doesn't happen. Sadly, those are the moments Jean pays her respects to a cozy spot on the corner of 17th Street and Avenue J, and it's not having coffee with Hannah, but somewhere within me.

Miss Jean occasionally becomes an unwelcome obsession — my uninvited guest, riffing and having her way in my head. That voice never leaving me entirely. And while I try to hush her, I realize there must be a purpose I haven't found. I've never told Hannah. It's probably for the better that I don't. She shouldn't have to shoulder that.

It's not possession. It's worse because it's within me. Some neurological breakdown in my wiring just waiting to short circuit at the wrong moment. I don't wish this on anyone. I've got no one to own up to but myself and you, whoever you are.

She's hovering in there, waiting to pounce in a troubled spot near my hippocampus, just standing on her little soapbox, queued up and ready to plague and irritate me — a microphone in hand with her greasy ponytail and Gonzo yapping next to her.

I look over at Hannah and smile as she rests peacefully.

No sleeping pills.

No Garashock.

No alcohol.

We've kicked our habits around here, and we're back in group therapy. The NA and AA mashup seemed a natural fit. Not so surprisingly, we see some of the same faces from Grief Support having crossed over because of an overenabling sponsor in the other group who also happens to be a member. No judgment, just real people, hoping and longing to connect and find accountability. That's all.

Real Jean's an overworked state employee I hired at a Denny's with a knack for method acting. Miss Jean hovers closer inside. Her wedge driven so deep I can't correct it. So, if a guy is this aware, what can he do? Get her the hell out of Dodge so it's just him again. I want to give that piece of real estate stolen from the attic of my mind back to its rightful owner. That's where we are now — me, you, and her. Telling you what you need to hear to know me and to get her out of the way. Miss Jean isn't welcome anymore and she shouldn't be with you either. It's with this we bid you proper farewell from 1737 17th Street, hoping and praying you never find yourself caught in such a miserable hell.

Godspeed.

# AUTHOR'S NOTE

Oh, Jeanie, my dear Jeanie,

Where do we start? Hopefully, me still in Texas, and you somewhere in Montana and never to meet again. If you never get this, that's okay with me. Yet, somehow, I'm certain it'll find its way.

Our written affair began in February when I wanted to run away. It didn't conclude until ten months later. I only thought I knew you. Until you confronted me in my dreams and told me I didn't, and that's where our real story started.

You lectured me on why I needed to know Hannah before I could know you. And then, once I proved I knew her, you told me I needed to know Ben the most. When I realized I knew Ben all along, you taught me I was nothing more than a pawn. A piece on your chessboard to play with and laugh at. I hope I gave you what you were looking for.

As I revisited our fling, I found there was more to us — teeth to our past I didn't want to remember. Long buried feelings I hoped to never find. Somehow, you reeled me in, trapping me, and making sure we'd meet again. Though I'm not ready to revisit you, I know you'll be waiting for me somewhere in the mountains of Montana, its frigid air waiting for our reunion.

Forever conflicted,
Dan McDowell

***

You know, this was a process. It was an adventure, but it took me to depths I never expected. I don't know that I could have anticipated that. It started on a whim. A comment from a neighbor the first time we met. A one-liner from a dad at a birthday party. A series of character studies I thought would orient me or help me find a groove, but, ultimately, it's just all those things culminating, the stress in my life, and an unrelenting imagination.

Before long, I was in another world not so foreign to my own but still its own distinct place. My mind, an unseen playground to explore, its rust and splinters included. The keys clicking and clacking beneath my fingertips, me compulsively saving them like they were plenary-inspired gold. My children screaming, squealing, and needing their father. My wife needing a husband. More than anything, me realizing I needed all of them.

Upon further review, I concluded I'd just rewrite this again and again and again until Miss Jean screamed at me to stop.

That seems to be a sort of sweet spot for most of us eccentric writer types, until we give up and say, enough, or someone else says, you're out of time, hand it over.

I know nothing of acting and little of writing, but I believe I went close to method here. A quick internet perusal tells me there is such a thing, so before I pat myself on the back for a remotely original thought, I'm grounded by the fact that ten thousand others have done this before me. Maybe even ten million. So now, I hibernate for the winter, hoping to thaw out in the spring, and when we all meet again, this amalgamation of words will hit the presses and you'll know why.

# SPECIAL THANKS

(In some particular order)

God.

The Oxford Comma.

My editor, Mark Levesque. You brought this to technicolor.

Magnolia Filling Station.

Wife, kids, mom, dad, brothers, sister, nephews, grandparents, aunts, uncles, in-laws, outlaws, cousins, readers, yaysayers, naysayers, and soothsayers.

To authors I've networked with and met along the way: Greg Hoover, Jeff Bailey, Jeffrey James Higgins, Jill Benson, Brian Jeffreys, Gojan Nikolich, Tom McCaffrey, Val Conrad, Joe Barrett, Steven Rigolosi, Kimberly Tilley, Kristin Sherry, Bob Zeidman, John Hunt, Lee Jordan, and Emily Miller.

To Black Rose Writing: Reagan, Chris, Minna, Justin, and Dave.

To the Beta Readers.

To Angie and Sean.

To second and third tier films, books, and television. Each of you holds a piece to a greater story that could be told. An influence that could have been memorable. Your story had the bones, and though it might have fallen flat just as mine could, you gave me fuel to walk alongside each of you in a parallel but asynchronous universe, and for this, I'm extremely grateful.

# ABOUT THE AUTHOR

Dan McDowell is a husband and father by day, and an author by night. The end result, chilling stories with gritty and real people facing unmistakable obstacles. With inspiration emerging from the best and the worst of Dan's nightmares, memories, and hyperactive imagination, he weaves tales of bizarre and intriguing proportions into a new stratosphere of descriptive writing that remains both distinct and thought provoking. He and his family currently reside in the San Antonio, TX, area.

# IF YOU HAVE TIME

Word-of-mouth is crucial for any author to succeed. If you enjoyed *When She Comes Knocking*, please leave a review online—anywhere you are able. Even if it's just a sentence or two. It would make all the difference and would be very much appreciated.

Thanks!
Dan McDowell

## CHECK OUT ANOTHER RELEASE FROM DAN MCDOWELL!

"The Shining meets Dante's Inferno... brimming with sinister surprises sure to keep horror fans up at night."
–*Best Thrillers*

Made in the USA
Columbia, SC
07 June 2023

17826729R00114